Boneya War

CW01499227

ACKNOWLEDGMENTS

I'd like to thank my wife Lori and my two daughters, CJ and Jackie, for putting up with me while I wrote this latest. Any similarities between people in this book and my immediate family and friends is purely intentional. Of course, I wouldn't be much of a pastor if I didn't acknowledge God – to Him be all the glory! To keep up to date on all my books... be sure to follow me on Amazon by clicking the +Follow button on my authors page!

Chapter 1: Dog Pound...

Did you ever wake up wondering where you were... and perhaps equally important, how you got there? Yeah, me too. The only the thing is, it usually happens when I've been drinking... and I'd been dry for the better part of two years.

I'm Commodore Jeremy David Riker... my friends call me JD or just plain "Dog." I have the dubious honor of running a starship boneyard in the middle of nowhere.

My head hurt and there was a funny smell. It was almost like ozone or something medicinal. I opened my eyes and then shut them real-quick. Carefully, I opened a single eyelid. I closed it again... real-quick.

You have to understand; I had been running this boneyard for the Federated Fleet for the better part of three years. That's what happens when you are an ambitious, up-and-coming, fleet officer and you piss off a Federation Admiral by marrying his only daughter... and then have the audacity to get separated from her when she insists you give up your command-track.

A man like me and a nice safe desk job don't mix. I tried to explain this to my wife... but all I got was a nasty letter and a promotion. Admiral 'Dad' dumped (I mean posted) me in the middle of nowhere. Most people who knew me eventually got royally pissed off with me. What can I say? It's a gift... the result of being too smart... too honest... too often.

I tried opening up my eyes a second time and then closed them just as fast... bummer. Nothing had changed.

Again, you have to understand... I knew the smell and look of every piece of dilapidated junk orbiting the Ceres boneyard. What I just saw... and what I had been smelling... didn't look like anything I remembered.

I had to make a decision. Do I open my eyes and deal with this situation? Or do I keep my eyes closed... go back to sleep and hope the problem goes away? In the end, my bladder forced an answer. I really had to pee.

I slowly opened my eyes. Yup... *Dorothy you're not in Kanas any more.*

I appeared to be in some type of geeky science lab. The lights were dim and had a distinct reddish cast to them. The equipment was like nothing I had ever seen before.

I mean it was clearly electronic, but nothing looked like anything I had ever run across … and being the top dog in a junkyard for interplanetary space ships meant I had pretty much run across everything good old Terra could make and fly in our solar system. Everything from state-of-the-art Chinese Zǎo- Shang destroyers fragged in that dust-up over Mars… to the really big Indian Shaktishaalee-Bal ships. We only had one of those – they're pretty damn tough to kill.

My point is, I had seen it all… and this wasn't anything I had seen.

I rolled off the padded table I had awoken on. It was then that I noticed that I was dressed the same way my momma brought me into the world… which was to say I was not. Now I was getting really pissed off.

My threads were a point of pride. I was only a captain in the Federated Fleet… but since I was the commander-of-record for more than one ship… (I had the command codes for over two hundred but I'm not bragging), I was technically allowed to wear a Commodore star above a gold band. It didn't change my paygrade but hey ya can't have everything.

With my uniform AWOL and a full bladder, I was beginning to wonder *just what I had gotten myself into?*

My last memory was taking a flitter to inspect a Mars Gnat fighter that had just been recovered and dropped off at the boneyard. They were a dime a dozen but sometimes they had unexploded ordnance that could be a real problem with the other boneyard ships orbiting Ceres. One little bang and I could spend weeks (and a year's fuel allotment) chasing down the strays that had been knocked out of orbit.

It seemed to me, as I was approaching the Gnat... yeah that's right! There had been something huge suddenly pop up on my LIDAR. The next thing I knew, I had a headache and a really full bladder.

That last was becoming a serious concern. I didn't see anything that looked like a head. I started to look for a bottle or a flask... or even a sink with a drain in it. I had finally decided on a corner, chosen at random if you're curious, when I heard a swish behind me.

"Oh, good you're awake."

I turned around, hands placed strategically to protect my honor.

The female voice sounded familiar. It was the voice of the person most responsible for my having that Commodore star. Lori Spratt, Admiral Spratt's one and only daughter.

***

It's amazing what an empty bladder, clean clothes, and a cup of reasonably good coffee can do to improve your outlook on life. The fact that a gorgeous blond was sitting across the table from me was an added plus.

We were in a sealed section of what seemed to be a ship of some type. The tech was vaguely familiar in that you could easily figure out the function… but at the same time the designs were like nothing I had ever seen before.

The areas we could explore included the med-bay I had awoken in, a small sleeping chamber, a constantly running stream-like bathtub and what appeared to be a galley which was our current location. Every other door was sealed and no amount of effort on my part seemed to be able to force them open. When I tried too hard, I received an electric shock that served to dissuade me.

Lori had shared that she had been locked in this same 'suite', for lack of a better term, for about six days.

"So, it's just you and me on this… whatever the hell it is we're on?" I asked for about the tenth time.

I was still wrapping my head around everything that had happened. It turned out Lori had been on an ambulance shuttle between Deep Space 4 and Lagrange 1 when something showed up on the LIDAR. The next thing she knew, she woke up stark naked and with a full bladder.

Here's the thing. I had been dating Lori for years. We got married and had a great life until I was offered a command-track. Command-tracks are hard to come by. I was stoked. Lori, not so much. My point is, I knew Lori. I knew something was up when I came home with the position announcement… and I knew something was up now.

The first time I had been foolish enough to ask her what was wrong. We ended up getting into a pretty serious fight. It ended in a legal separation. Neither one of us wanted to fully give up on the marriage yet.

This time was different. We were on, what I had to assume, was an alien ship... there was no other way to reconcile the equipment we were seeing and all the little oddities... like chairs that were just a little too small and lights that weren't quite the right shade.

I figured we were pretty screwed as it was, so, there really was nothing to lose by asking her to spill the beans. There was something she was not telling me. I could see it in her eyes.

I took a big swig of coffee and cleared my throat.

She knew my 'tells' and started to speak before I could ask the question we both knew I was about to ask.

"I didn't think he would do it," she sobbed. "I told him that you were in command of the biggest Earth fleet."

"Didn't think... who... he?" I asked a bit confused. It seemed like there was a piece missing here.

"The Archon," she said finally. "He's the AI that runs this ship. He was sent on a mission to recruit command staff."

"I'll bite... recruit for who?"

"Perhaps I should be the one to answer that."

I fell out of my seat trying to spin around so fast. I'm pretty attuned to my environment. People don't sneak up on me. It's almost as if I can hear the air move sometimes. It freaked out the other cadets during combat simulations. Nobody ever got the drop on the Dog. It just didn't happen.

All that said, I didn't hear or sense a thing, and all of a sudden there is a 'five foot nothing' kid standing not three feet from my six. Well, kid is probably the wrong term. It was a freak'n alien… with a big fat capital A!

The oddest thing, aside from the small grey feathers and the fact that it looked more like an otter than anything else, was the deep – James Earl Jones—voice. For those that don't get the reference, Jones was an actor circa mid-twentieth to early twenty-first century. He was the voice of that classic pre-holographic Scifi called Star Jedi or something like that. My point is… this critter… and I'm assuming it was the ship's AI, had a really deep voice.

There is only one thing an otter with a deep voice can mean… you got it… more coffee! There were any number of possibilities that could explain what I was seeing.

First, this could be the mother of all hangover dreams. Still, I hadn't been drinking for the better part of two years.

Second, it was possible that the CO_2 scrubbers on my ship were on the fritz. On the other hand, my shipsuit would have warned me and automatically engaged a series of backups. I can't remember, outside of a simulation in boot camp, where both a scrubber and its backups had failed.

The third option… the one that I was having the hardest time swallowing… was that this was real. Without any real choice; I decided to go with option three and see where it led me.

"You would be the Archon?" I asked.

"That is correct," the alien answered.

"Are you real? Can I touch you?"

"The first is most certainly true. The second is not possible. I am constructed of artificially coalesced photons… what you would call a hologram. I serve as the avatar for the AI that controls this survey ship."

"Woooh," I said as my hand passed through the little guy's chest.

"As I indicated, I am currently a holographic being," the Archon answered.

"OK, I believe you. That being the case," I added, "I'm going to assume you know a lot more about what is going on than I do. I don't suppose you be willing to fill in some of the gaps?"

The *little grey otter alien Archon holographic thingy* walked over to an empty chair at the table, pulled it out and sat in it. There were two things here that caused me to raise an eyebrow. First the chair was exactly *'little grey otter alien Archon holographic thingy'* size… and second, I had just established that the bloody bugger was non-corporeal. How the hell did it manage to touch the chair… much less pull it away from the table?

I looked at Lori and started to open my mouth, but the Archon spoke first.

"As you have undoubtedly surmised, I have the ability to interact with the physical world by the judicious use of micro-force field emitters distributed throughout the ship."

"Undoubtedly," I agreed, a little tongue-in-cheek.

The otter looked at me and wrinkled its nose. I'm not sure what that meant in *alien otter,* but I suspect it was his way of saying he doubted the veracity of my statement.

"About that whole 'clueing me in to whatever the hell it is that is going on' thing..."

"Yes. I suppose we should... what's that English phrase? ...*bring you up to speed*. I am an Archon. My name would be difficult for you to pronounce but you may call me Mephibosheth."

"Ma-fib-o-what?" I said. "How about I call you Mitty and we just leave it at that?"

The otter wrinkled its nose again... I really was going to need to figure out what that meant.

"Mitty is acceptable," the alien finally replied. "I am an Archon. My entire race excels at political leadership. That is in fact our role in the Galactic Order. There are members of the Galactic Order that excel in medicine, engineering, art, history, logic and any number of other things."

"So, there is a whole intergalactic community out there," I mumbled. It was time for another sip of coffee.

"Technically, we would be considered a galactic community because, as-of-yet we do not have any member-states from outside our own galaxy," Mitty corrected me.

"I stand corrected."

"You are sitting."

"Don't go there Mitty," I warned. "I've got a bad headache and have not had anywhere near enough coffee, yet. How about you share why you and I are having this conversation… beyond the fact that I asked you to fill in the gaps."

"We seek the services of a race that excels at *military* leadership."

Ok, I have to admit… I didn't see that one coming.

Chapter 2: Not your average Dog…

"I'll bite. Why come here? Why come to the Sol system?"

Mitty squirmed in his seat. "Perhaps I need to share a bit more of the specifics of our situation."

"Go for it little guy," I said with a wave of my hand.

I could tell by the look that Lori was giving me, that she was not a fan of my flippant attitude… but hey… I had been kidnapped. Besides, I was on a roll. What more could the little guy do to me… actually, as I thought about it… there was quite a lot he could do. Maybe flippant wasn't such a good play.

Mitty wiped his hand/paw over the tabletop and a really neat holographic display magically appeared. These guys had some seriously cool tech.

The Archon pressed a few holographic buttons and a three-dimensional star map appeared, floating above the table. Did I mention all the really cool tech stuff these guys had?

"This is a display of star systems under control of the Galactic Order as of two of your Earth years ago." Mitty pressed a few more virtual buttons. "This is the current state-of-affairs."

The change was dramatic. It looked like something on the order of twenty or so star systems had changed from blue to orange on the map.

I moved closer to the display. "May I?" I made to rotate the display. I had seen the set of gestures Mitty had used and I was pretty sure I had the fundamentals down.

"By all means, Commodore Riker," the alien said.

I rotated the display. It seemed the areas in orange were on opposite sides of the sphere of influence controlled by the Galactic Order.

"You're either dealing with multiple attackers or one coordinated attacker intent on dividing up your forces," I said.

"You are correct," Mitty confirmed. "Our defense forces are in a state of disarray. The first battle took place in a star system called Gilboa. The indigenous people were called the Saulites. They were military geniuses that helped to keep the peace for tens of hundreds of your years."

"You used the past-tense," I said. "What happened at the battle of Gilboa?"

"Our enemy used a mutagenic virus tailored to eradicate the entire Saulite species. By the time we knew what had happened the contagion had spread to every corner of our empire. There were no survivors."

I turned to look at Mitty. What I saw was a very human emotion in his face. I don't know if his AI algorithms were aping a facial expression I would recognize or if the Archon race simply emoted in the same way we did. The bottom line was the idea of complete genocide meant, if what we were being told was true, that this 'enemy' was ruthless in the extreme.

Lori chose that moment to ask a question. "Who exactly is your enemy?"

Mitty's head turned slightly to face her more directly. "We don't know. What we do know is that their initial attack was perfectly executed and destroyed our military command and control structure. Their second attack attempted to destroy our governmental institutions. It almost succeeded but our medical personnel identified what was happening and isolated my homeworld before the contagion could spread."

I heard a sharp intake of breath and realized it was me that had made the noise.

"Are you saying your homeworld has been decimated?"

Mitty sighed in what was again an all-too-human response.

"No, Commodore. A decimation would imply a one-tenth reduction in our population. The death toll on my homeworld of Lo Debar was just shy of one hundred percent. In point of fact, it was in my spouse's arms that I died... having watched all twelve of our children pass first."

"My God," I said softly. I began to understand what motivated this AI. If Mitty's algorithms were capable of one percent the anguish I would have felt in a similar situation, the Archon AI would move the heavens themselves to put a stop to what was going on.

I stood up and went over to the wall-mounted dispenser and put my coffee cup under the spigot. I still had half a cup left but the walking gave my mind a chance to digest what I was hearing. The coffee had been a source of endless fascination for me. It as well as most of the food on the ship was completely, but accurately, recreated synthetically from samples acquired from around the solar system. I shook my head and got back to the conversation at hand.

"Your military command and control is wiped out. Your normal governmental hierarchy is, at the very least, severely disrupted… meaning your logistics are disrupted. Several things are abundantly clear."

I walked back over to the table and once again rotated the holographic star map.

"First, whoever is responsible… is intimately familiar with the structure and inherent weaknesses of your Galactic Order. Second, they also are ruthless in ways that boggle the mind. Third, they are either a powerful dictatorship or a race much more similar to humanity than the member worlds of your Galactic Order… or both."

The Archon stood up and walked towards a door that had been sealed.

"I would be curious to know how you deduced the last," the alien said.

I took a big swig of the coffee I had been drinking. If I was right, Lori and I were about to be released from our prison.

"Genocide is a ruthless tactic. It's hard to believe any type of galactic coalition of planets could survive if its members were known to be willing to use such harsh tactics. That means the race that is attacking is able to either force its member states to cooperate in despicable behavior… or that race is like humanity and adept at a large number of disparate disciplines. As an example. My wife," I pointed towards Lori, "is one of the finest physicians in the fleet. I, on the other hand, am just a military man."

"Your logic is faultless. You also appear to have a degree of humility. This too is a positive."

"Humility?"

The little grey otter did that nose thing again.

"Perhaps I used the wrong word. You are, undoubtedly, one of the finest leaders in your Federation as witnessed by your personal command of the fleet with the largest number of ships in your solar system. Your aptitude scores were among the best in the history of your command academy. Both your peers and your instructors have consistently given you the highest ratings. I confirmed these facts prior to cloning you.

"In light of this information, to use the phrase, 'just a military man' would indicate a certain degree of self-depreciation commonly referred to as humility... is it not?"

"About that whole fleet thing," I started to say before the last part of what the Archon said registered completely. I paused as my mind digested the implications.

"Did I hear you right... you've made a copy of me?" I said bewildered. "Why in God's green Earth would you do that? Where is this clone and what are you going to do with it?"

"Commodore, you misunderstand. You are the copy... as is your spouse. We will be gone for an extended period of time and your disappearance would raise questions that would be better if they did not get asked"

"And if Lori and I decide not to go with you? What then?"

"I calculated a 98.942 percent chance that you would agree to go with me as our military advisor before I began the replication process."

"I see… you somehow calculated that there was only one chance in a hundred that I'd say no." Let me state for the record, I hate being manipulated. This alien otter was pressing some buttons on my psyche that were best left un-pressed.

"Technically one point zero-five-eight," the otter corrected.

I started to get really pissed off but then I realized the little bugger had me. As much as I hate being manipulated… I hated it more when the manipulator succeeded. There was no way I was backing out of this.

There were three factors that made saying no just about impossible. First, this was a chance to go where no man had gone before. Second, there was some seriously neat tech here. Finally, and perhaps most importantly, I wasn't sure I could walk away from the genocide that was going on. I had always been the 'anti-bully' in school. It was just part of the way I was wired.

"Let us not love with words or speech but with actions and in truth," I muttered softly.

Mitty twitched his nose and opened the previously sealed door he was standing next too. He had obviously determined I had accepted my fate. Did I mention the little bugger was pissing me off?

* * *

The *Gilboa*, named in honor of the race that had sacrificed their last soul towards the defense of the Galactic Order, was a big ship. It dwarfed the combined mass of the entire Terran fleet. That said, it was a mess.

It seemed the, as yet unidentified nefarious enemy, had taken umbrage to her mission to scout for races that could assist in the defense of the Galactic Order. The ship's entire crew had been killed during the battle that had ensued.

The ship's AI, Mitty, had managed to activate the ship's FTL drive at the last possible second. Sadly, critical components had failed just after emergence from an artificial Einstein-Rosen bridge. This presented us with a problem. How do you fix a ship this big without spare parts?

Fortunately, I knew of a guy who ran the biggest starship boneyard in the Terran system. I also knew of some of the best retired engineers ever to walk the decks of a starship. The question was how to recruit them?

I wasn't a fan of the kidnap and clone approach used by the Archon AI. He and I argued for the better part of a day about it before I simply crossed my arms and refused to discuss the matter further. I learned a very valuable lesson. AI's can get pissed off too. That said, Mitty finally relented. I was allowed to make direct contact and discuss the situation with several key individuals.

Lori spent her time, while Mitty and I were having our little spat, checking out and reconfiguring the ship's larger med bay. As expected, the Galactic Order's medical tech was nothing to sneeze at. Lori's discoveries ended up providing me some incentives for the team I was hoping to recruit.

My first acquisition was an old codger named Whiskers McGraw. Whiskers was about as good an engineer as they ever made. He was flirting with the high side of ninety but between rejuv treatments and living in a low gravity environment so far away from the sun... he could have passed for a man twenty-years younger.

Many times, when ships would come into the boneyard, they would be deader than a doornail. We'd tow them to where we needed them to be... if we had to. I always preferred to park them with at least minimally working reaction or VASMR drives because it made keeping them where they were supposed to be that much easier. Commander William McGraw (ret) was my go-to guy for getting most of these derelicts semi-operational.

To my way of thinking, they broke the mold after they made him. He forgot, on a daily basis, more engineering stuff than most people learned in a lifetime. He could listen to a fusion core and tell you which induction points were most likely to fail next. If there was anybody alive who was going to get the *Gilboa* flying again at FTL speeds... it was Whiskers.

Mitty had given me a three-hour block of instruction on how to use the Gilboa's communication hardware. I put the training to good use as I reached out to my buddy. It was Friday night, so I knew Whiskers would be at the card table teaching the youngsters, as he liked to call us, how to lose money to an old engineer.

"Whiskers, ya got your ears on buddy?"

A few seconds later a familiar voice responded, "I got ya five by five. What's up Commodore?"

"Well, I'm afraid I can't say over an open line. Any chance you'd be willing to look at a derelict and give it some of your tender loving care? It's a bit of a special challenge."

"I'll need another ten or fifteen minutes to finish learn'n these youngsters the meaning of humility, then I'm all yours."

"Funny you should mention 'humility'… I have someone for you to meet that is a big fan of humility. Meet me at zone sixteen and I'll show you what I'm interested in having you take a look at."

Chapter 3: Some Dogs have all the luck…

"I gotta hand it to ya, Commodore. When you said, 'special challenge', alien hardware is not the first thing that came to mind. How'd you find this thing?"

"It found me. I woke up on this thing three days ago. There's an AI that runs the ship. It seems there is a war going on and they need our help. The other side is engaging in complete and absolute genocide… and not just of an isolated population center but of entire species."

Whiskers shook his head. "Sonny, what you're saying done'a track with reality. I spoke with you, in person, not four hours ago. You was going on about how this was your anniversary and how you wished you could patch things up with the old lady. If yer mistaken about the one, how can I trust ya about the other?"

Lori chose that moment to walk into the engineering compartment I had been showing the Commander.

"Old lady?" She said with a smile on her face. Whiskers was practically an uncle to her. The engineer had worked closely with her father for almost her entire life.

"Missy! Good gravy. Sonny brought you all the way out here and didn't say a word to me. It's enough to hurt a man's feelings… it is."

"About that," I said carefully. "Neither Lori nor I are actually here. Well we are here… but we are not actually ourselves. Well, we are ourselves but not the 'ourselves' you think we are."

"It's confusing," Lori added. "The easiest way to say it is…"

"We're clones," I blurted out.

Whiskers rubbed his chin. "Cloning is illegal."

"Tell that to the Archon," I said. "It's not like he asked our permission before he did it."

"So, the Dog I had lunch with…"

"…is the real Commodore Riker," I confirmed. "He doesn't even know he's been cloned. The same is true for Lori."

Whiskers whistled. "Ya don't say. And me… are ya planning to clone me too?"

"Absolutely not! Mitty and I had quite an argument about the ethics of what he did to Lori and me. We have all the memories and feelings of our originals but no way to step back into our lives. I convinced him…"

Lori snorted.

"OK, I demanded that we recruit people the old-fashioned way. We ask them to join us."

"So, you're asking me to join you?" Whiskers said with a bit of wonder in his voice.

I nodded. "I'd very much like you to be part of this… whatever this is. As far as I can tell the pay is terrible and there will be aliens all over the place. What'd ya say?"

Whiskers grinned from ear to ear. "Commodore, ya had me at 'aliens'. I ain't no spring chicken but if an old man can help ya… I can't think of a better way to spend my last days."

Lori chuckled. "I might have a few surprises for you in the med-bay."

***

Six days later Whiskers had managed to recruit ten more old timers. Two were mathematicians, one was a cook. Another two were retired nurses and the rest were either engineers or operations officers. Not a one of them was under the age of eighty.

That's where Lori's surprise in the med-bay was especially useful. It seemed the Galactic Order was much better at tissue rejuvenation then backwater places like the Sol system. Lori had the entire volunteer team on a treatment regimen that Mitty confirmed would have them back in their prime in less than a year. Already, Whiskers had a spring in his step that I hadn't ever remembered seeing.

Mitty gave me operational control of the ship. He functioned as my executive officer and technical advisor.

I put Commander McGraw in charge of engineering and assigned the two other engineers, Sandy Heinz and the unfortunately named John a.k.a. 'Jack' Daniels to assist him. Everybody else was assigned to learn ships systems and to help prioritize repairs.

Ten days into the repair process we ran into our first major glitch. The active shielding effectively cloaked the ship from Federation sensors. This allowed us to work undisturbed. We harvested materials from my boneyard which the *Gilboa's* fabricators were able to use to build replacement components. The work was made doubly hard because most of the systems we were repairing were completely unfamiliar at even the most basic technical level. It was like trying to fix a lightbulb when you didn't even know what electricity was.

The glitch we ran into involved the active shielding. To fix one of the essential systems, we would have to shut it down for several hours. Normally, given the vastness of space, this would not be a problem but some overly ambitious Commodore... who shall remain unnamed... put a massive sensor net in place to detect errant asteroids that could potentially disrupt the boneyard. What can I say... I was bored and wanted to do more than just sit at a desk and ponder my fate.

That sensor net would light up like a Christmas tree the moment we shut down our shields. The problem was ultimately solved by creating a distraction. We used small charge to blow up one of the Gnats in a parking orbit around Ceres. The resulting disruption send a dozen ships into motion. These in turn collided with a handful of other ships. The original Commodore Riker would have his hands full for a while. I felt bad about it because I took great pride in excelling at whatever job I was given... even if I hated it with every fiber of my being. Strangely I found myself in the position of hoping I could forgive myself at some future point.

***

Later that same day, Whiskers came up to me in utter frustration. I had asked for a status update. The ship's AI had been evasive when it came to giving me said estimate. That evasiveness took the form of cryptic statements regarding the amount of risk we would be willing to take.

When I asked for clarification, the little grey otter shut up tighter than a sphincter during a proctology exam. Ergo the meeting with Commander McGraw.

"Commodore, as far as I can tell, it's going to take us darn near a couple of years to get this boat going. It's not that the work is hard... it's just none of my guys has any clue what we're doing."

He waved his hand around the entire engineering department. "All this stuff is based on science we've barely begun to theorize about... much less master. It's like asking a Roman Centurion to fix an internal combustion engine. He knows all about fire, combustibles and even to a limited degree... things that go bang... but would you hand him the key fob to your vintage 2055 Lamborghini?"

"I understand all that," I said. "Isn't the Archon AI assisting you?"

"Abs-sa-freaking-lutely sir. But imagine having to do a surgery with the guy holding the knife having to ask the only surgeon in the room to explain in detail the ins and outs of each and every step. There's a good chance of the patient dying of old age on the table."

I sighed and walked around one of the partially disassembled engineering consoles. I picked up a piece of something that looked vaguely electronic. I had no clue what it did or where it went. I didn't know if it was functional in its current state... hell, it might well be a tool and not part of the disassembled console at all. I put the thingy-ma-bob down.

"So, we have a problem. What's the solution?"

Whiskers shook his head. "Damned if I know, Sir. Damned if I know."

"OK, do the best you can. I'm going to have a heart-to-virtual-heart with our little grey friend."

"Thank you, Sir. Me and my boys are going to do our best for ya... I just wanted you to know what we're up against."

"Understood, Engineer. Carry on."

***

I had intended to speak with Mitty again, but Lori paged me to the med-bay. She sounded excited. I needed some good news, so I put off contacting the ship's AI until I had a chance to talk with Lori.

I had to admit, having her, even a clone of her, back in my life was the best thing that had happened to me in years. We were still living in separate quarters, but the old wounds were healing. Neither one of us had stopped loving the other and in my mind, defective though it is, that boded well for the future.

The med-bay was up two decks from engineering. Whiskers had gotten the antigravity turbo shafts working three days ago so the trip to see my gal was a quick one.

I walked into the bay and was greeted with the biggest, broadest smile I had seen since the day I had proposed to her. I looked around the room, but I didn't see anything more unusual than normal.

"What's up Doc?"

By way of answer, she walked over to me and planted the biggest and best kiss I had had in years straight on my lips. In such a situation, a man has only a limited number of options. I kissed her back. The kiss lasted for several minutes and at some point, completely of their own volition, my hands worked their way down to her rump... which I might add, was a very fine rump. I had always counted myself a very lucky man... until I wasn't. Now it seemed like there might be hope for us yet.

Lori leaned into the kiss a little harder and then reluctantly pulled away with a twinkle in her eye. "There will be time for that later soldier," she said. "I have something to show you that will change everything."

I was still focused on the 'time for that later' thing so I missed what she did next, but a door that had been frozen shut opened. Inside the room were a bunch of beauty salon chairs, complete with those little hair dryer helmets that fit over your head.

"OK..." I began. "So, you can get a permanent now," I added with, what I'm sure, was a quizzical look on my face.

Lori slapped me lightly on the back of my head, as if to say "engage your brain, dummy."

"The main crew of this ship were hairless and even the Archons had feathers. These aren't hair dryers, and this isn't some type of beauty salon." Lori turned to face me. "Did you ever wonder how Mitty managed to transfer our memory engrams to our cloned bodies?"

Now, I'm a reasonably bright guy... and in my defense, waking up on an alien battleship can be distracting... but no

I had never pondered that question. It made sense though. Cloning just involved replicating tissue. Memories were not part of the process... so something more had to be involved.

At that point, a cough behind me told me that our friendly neighborhood otter had holographically popped in for a visit.

***

So, it turns out the Archons had access to some rather sophisticated engrammatic transfer equipment. They were essentially teaching machines that could transfer an entire personality down to the last hiccup or selected skills. In the process, the machines remapped select neural pathways... which was a fancy way of saying that not only did the machines impart knowledge, but they also augmented basic intelligence.

This presented me with a problem. The reason Mephibosheth, a.k.a. Mitty, had kept this particular facility hidden was that it would force us to make a choice. If we chose to cross a line, there would be no going back. I understood the Archon's reasoning and I found myself agreeing with it.

Until we got more of the ship repaired and re-pressurized, the engine room was the largest open space we had. I called the crew together. It was time everybody knew what the score was.

"OK, gang... pipe down for a few minutes. I want to thank each of you for the job you've been doing. I know it's frustrating working on systems you don't understand and often don't even recognize."

There was a low grumble that traveled through the men and women in the room. Including Mitty, there were fourteen of us altogether.

"This is what I want to talk to each of you about. We have an answer to the problem... but it will require a sacrifice from anyone that wants to take advantage of it."

"What type of sacrifice are ya talking about Commodore?" Whiskers was the one asking the question.

I straightened my tunic and looked each of the assembled crew in the eyes. "It means you can never go home," I said simply.

There was quite a bit of additional muttering... which I had expected. I waited for it to die down.

"The bottom line is this. There are teaching machines near the med bay that can give us the knowledge and skills we need to operate and repair this ship. There are two things you need to know before agreeing to use these teaching machines however.

"You will have access to technology that the human race is probably not in a position to handle responsibly yet. This is why the Galactic Order forbids the dissemination of certain technologies to societies that do not yet have FTL technology. Mitty is violating the law by offering us access to this tech. If he doesn't, the Galactic Order will probably cease to exist. If he does... well let's hope the ends justify the means in this particular case.

"The second thing you should be aware of is the process can be painful but will also likely result in a modest increase in your IQ."

"So, what are we talking about here?"

I shrugged my shoulders. "Mitty?"

The Archon otter stepped up on a piece of equipment, so he could see the crowd.

"My species is bi-sentient. What that means is the males and females of my species have very different intelligent quotients. The females are the creators and inventors. The typical unenhanced female would be a borderline genius on your world. The males, on the other hand, hunt and dig holes for our families to live in. As a male, my IQ would normally be something on the order of 75 to 80 as you measure it. After cognitive enhancement treatments I tested at roughly one hundred and ten."

This was the first time I had heard these numbers. I have to admit I was shocked.

"You'll forgive me but that's a pretty average score for around here. You struck me as more intelligent than the average bear... or otter as the case may be."

Mitty wrinkled his nose again. One day I would learn what that meant. "I am currently running as an emulated being in the ship's computer core. My effective IQ would be off any meaningful human scale."

Chapter 4: Let sleeping Dogs lie…

In the end, every last one of the crew agreed to undergo the procedure. Sadly, this is what led to my very first fight with Lori since we had gotten back together.

As the captain, I felt it was my responsibility to vet any risk to the crew. I figured I had already been under the helmet… even if I didn't remember it… when my consciousness had been cloned from version 1.0 of me.

Lori didn't see it that way.

"Of all the bone-headed, imbecilic, stupid and just plain dumb things you could do… this has to take the cake," she screamed.

We were standing in the med bay. Whiskers and Mitty were standing with us. Mitty looked like… well like Mitty. Nothing ever seemed to phase the otter… beyond that nose thing he did.

Whiskers, on the other hand, had a grin that threaten to break his face. It was obvious that he was enjoying the show. I do have to admit… Lori was very attractive when she was passionate… and trust me when I say… she was passionate.

After several minutes questioning the nature of my genetic heritage, she finally stopped to catch her breath.

I started to open my mouth, but she held up a single forefinger. I had learned long ago that when the finger came up the only winning strategy was to shut up and just endure what was coming. Whiskers' soft chuckle was not helping.

"I am the medical doctor. I will go first for what is essentially a medical procedure and that is the end of it. Period."

She crossed her arms and dared me to contradict her. Surprisingly, I was saved from a fate worse than death by my good buddy Commander Whiskers McGraw.

"Beggin the lady's pardon. But as the only doctor on board... it would make more sense if you were not first into the barn. If things go south for the winter... you may be the only one who can operate the snow shovel... if ya get my drift."

I was always amazed at Whiskers' ability to create and disseminate the oddest metaphors at a moment's notice.

"Surely you're not suggesting that JD goes first!"

"Absolutely not Missy. I'm the logical choice," Whiskers responded with a smug grin. "Go ahead. Ask me why."

"OK, why?" Lori and I asked in unison.

"Right now, you need an engineer. Ya ain't got one. I am about useless other than the simple fact that I can pull and push and turn and twist when Otter-boy tells me too. Anybody can do that. If this fails on me... ya lose nothing but a guy that can beat ya in cards. If it succeeds, ya get a fixed starship."

Mitty turned to Lori and I. "His logic is impeccable. Although the risk of something bad happening is minimal, the reality is we do not have a lot of experience training your species. Mister Whiskers would be the better choice."

* * *

Twenty minutes later the Commander was strapped in the chair with the cranial helmet placed over his head. Mitty began the procedure.

"I must warn you again Mister Whiskers. The procedure has the potential to be mildly uncomfortable. The more neural pathways that get optimized the greater the potential for discomfort."

I was curious. "Mitty, how does the system determine the need to 'optimize' neural pathways? Is it based on what needs to be learned or something else?"

"That is an insightful question, Commodore. There are two aspects of knowledge transfer. The first is a simple implantation of the relevant information. If the subject has a brain that is sufficiently capacious, this is never a problem. The second factor that the training system addresses is the subject's ability to efficiently utilize the information. The system analyzes the subject's brain structure and decides how much potential there is for improvement. The more gifted the individual is to begin with the more likely additional improvement will be possible."

I looked at Whiskers again. He was my friend and I didn't want to see any harm come to him. I debated overruling the others and taking the seat like I had originally planned. In the end, I did not. At a certain point you had to trust the wisdom of the people around you. In addition, they had to know that they had your trust, or you would never get the best out of them.

Whiskers gave me a thumbs-up. "I'm hungry guys and gals... lets scramble some eggs!"

Mitty brought up a holographic control panel and began to work the controls like a maestro at the Philharmonic Orchestra. Whiskers stiffened in the chair. His fingers extended sharply and then they relaxed, somewhat.

"Wow," the older man said. "That's worse than a hangover from Smitty's moonshine."

"Please sit still and try not to move. The procedure has a few more minutes to run before it is complete," the Archon AI said.

About five minutes later the straps on the chair automatically released Whiskers and the helmet retracted.

Whiskers just sat there for a few minutes breathing deeply.

"Well," he said at last while he stepped out of the chair. "That was certainly interesting. I definitely feel different. There's still a lot that I don't understand about how this ship operates but it's almost as if the core concepts are on the tip of my tongue."

"It will take several days or weeks before your brain has fully integrated the new engrams. You will slowly be able to access more and more of the information that was imparted to you. To use an expression native to your home world... You appear to have weathered the experience with flying colors."

Lori stepped forward with a device that looked like the Galactic Order version of a medical tricorder. "You'll forgive me if I run a few checks myself... Doctor Mitty," Lori said with just a little irritation in her voice. I don't think she had forgiven the little grey otter for siding with the engineer in the debate over who should go first.

I made to sit in the chair, but Lori gave me that patented look that females give to men about to engage in an activity they disapprove of. I knew that I would never hear the end of it, if I did not let her go next. I decided that losing a single battle was better than losing the whole war.

Lori's experience in the chair was not much different from the Engineer's. I suspect that she had a higher tolerance for pain... or she was at least better able to mask it. When she stepped out of the chair she had the biggest smile on her face. She looked around the teaching room as well as the small med bay.

"It's so clear now," she said. "I know what all of this equipment does. This is amazing!"

"Mitty," I said turning towards the ship's AI. "It feels like Lori has a faster and fuller grasp of her new engrams than Commander McGraw. Is the rate of assimilation different between individuals?"

"Affirmative, Commodore. Your spouse had a slightly better capacity for optimization. This has resulted in a faster assimilation of the implanted engrams. You should know that most species take considerably longer in incorporate these lessons then your people are demonstrating. It would appear that humans are especially suited to this type of knowledge enhancement. That bodes well for our prospects of ultimately being successful."

"OK, my turn," I said.

Whiskers shook his head. "Begg'n the Commodore's pardon... but unless you are planning on crawling through the duct work of this beastie... It would be better to run my engineers through first. If this training system breaks down like three quarters of the rest of the systems in this ship... ya going to need them to fix it."

Two hours later, it was finally my turn. Mitty explained that I would receive complete operational specs on the *Gilboa*. I would be able to run any station and would even be able to work on the engines if I needed to. He also pointed out that because of the massive amount of data that was going to be dumped inside of my noggin... there was a good chance that it would take me months to fully assimilate it.

My thinking was the sooner we began... the sooner we would be done. I have to admit that Sandy Heinz's experience with the system had me a little concerned. She experienced more than just a little discomfort. The pain was so great she nearly bit through her tongue. Apparently, the training system had determined she had the potential to receive quite a bit of cognitive enhancement. At the end of the procedure, Mitty estimated her IQ in the one sixty to one seventy range. I had an IQ of one forty-three and was used to being the smartest person in the room. I guess that was no longer going to be true.

As I sat in the chair, its restraints closed over my arms. I have to admit to a certain degree of 'antsy-ness.' I was not a fan of being restrained. On the other hand, I was not a fan of having my noggin scrambled like yesterday's omelet if I moved too much. I decided the restraints, as distasteful as they might be, were probably a good idea.

"Let'r rip," I said with more bravado than I was feeling. It turns out my words were prophetic.

My entire skull felt warm. As odd as it might sound, I imagined it must be what it felt like to put your head in a microwave. Now to be clear, I did not derive a lot of comfort from that particular thought.

I was just at the point of thinking... this isn't so bad... when my world exploded. The pain was beyond anything I ever imagined. It was beyond anything I thought possible to imagine. I heard Lori screaming... something about 'breaking an arm.' There was an intense bright and all-consuming light behind my eyes. I could hear the sound of a thousand trains thundering in my ears. Every fiber of every nerve in my body was on fire.

All I know is the pain in my head drove me to the brink of madness... and perhaps a little bit beyond. Thankfully, after what seemed like hours of torment, I passed out. I didn't care if I ever woke up again. The pain was gone.

***

"He's waking up."

I have no idea who 'he' was but I wished they would be quiet. I had the mother of all hangovers and I needed my beauty sleep.

"His vitals are back into more reasonable ranges. The bone in his arm is knitting nicely. If I hadn't seen it with my own eyes, I would never have believed a man could do that to himself."

The voice was familiar. I liked the voice. It was a voice I could enjoy waking up to every day. I decided I wanted to see the owner of that angelic voice. I opened my eyes and was rewarded with a beautiful smile on the face of the loveliest woman I had ever seen.

"You're a pretty lady," I said with a throat that felt like it had been on the wrong end of a shouting match with a freight train.

"Water?"

The gorgeous blond held a small sippy cup to my lips. I remembered suddenly that her name was Lori.

"Just a sip. You've had a rough time of it," she cautioned in a gentle voice.

"Ya gave us a bit of a scare there, Commodore," Whiskers said. I was beginning to fit the pieces of my mind back into place. I knew that Commander 'Whiskers' McGraw was my chief engineer.

"The ship? The crew... OK?" I whispered.

Lori smiled. "He's going to be fine. He's already more concerned about his command than he is himself."

I closed my eyes again. It was time to let sleeping Dogs lie.

Chapter 5: Fixing the Dog house…

In hindsight… which is often my best view, I was glad I had not used the Da'Tellen Transfer device first. That was the proper name for the machine we had been using to train the new crew of the *Gilboa*. If we had, it's unlikely I would have survived and it's a certainty that none of the others would have risked using the trainer.

I had successfully integrated the entire "command package" in a little less than a week. Mitty confirmed that this was an accomplishment that was unparalleled in Galactic Order history. I wish I could take credit for it, but I was just lucky to have great genes and apparently an unparalleled ability to flop like a dying fish on the beach.

The 'discomfort' of the experience resulted in a broken arm as my muscles literally attempted to tear my body a part. Tissue regenerators, expertly applied by the lovely Doctor Lori Riker, repaired most of the self-inflicted damage before I even woke up. For those who are interested, I was in a coma for two full days.

There were several plus sides to my misadventures. I now knew more about the *Gilboa* than anybody currently alive. I was fully briefed on the adversary that we would be facing. If anything, Mitty had been sugar-coating the situation with the war. The unknown adversary ignored all pleas for mercy and offers to surrender. When their swarms of ships arrived in a system they established a complete and impenetrable interdiction zone… before beginning strategic bombing of large cities. These were the lucky races. Those like the homeworlds of the Archons or Saulites were simply wiped clean of all sentient life.

The other advantages to my newly tuned brain was an IQ that exceeded 180 and perhaps much more importantly… a final and complete reconciliation with my wife.

It had been a week since we had begun repairs on the ship in earnest. Every day, Whiskers and his engineering team became a little more adept with the systems they were working with and repairing.

I even rolled up my sleeves and pitched in. I could handle a charge-reduced inductive coupler with the best of them. What was even stranger… I knew what I was doing. I had to admit… as if I hadn't before… Galactic Order tech was amazing.

I was crawling through one of the connecting tubes in engineering that we had nicknamed 'Jefferies' tubes after a 1960's TV show. It was cramped and despite being a trim and fit thirty-two-year-old… I was getting tired squirming thru the duct. The systems had been designed for smaller creatures than the average hairless ape from Earth. In point of fact, the systems had been designed and built by the J'ni.

They were about twice the size of the Archons and looked like a cross between a badger and a raccoon. One evening, when I had showed Lori a holovid of them in action, she had gotten very excited and asked if we could get one for a pet. I explained they were sentient beings and had built the *Gilboa*. She bit her lower lip and pouted.

"I guess that means no," she had said.

I spent the rest of the night making it up to her. We didn't really get much sleep but hey… sometimes a man has to make sacrifices in order to insure domestic tranquility… and trust me on this… Lori was worth the sacrifice!

I bring all of this up because the system I was fixing in that Jefferies tube was going to fix the environmental systems in the last large section of the ship. The end result of which would mean we would finally have unfettered access to the entire interior of the ship.

The hull plating which had been breached in some of the previous fighting had been carefully repaired by Whiskers and his team in EVA suits several days before. We had hoped, at that point, to gain access to those areas of the ship, but the environmental glitch meant we could not replenish the air supply in that section of the ship. No amount of advanced tech in the universe would allow you to breath hard vacuum so we were forced to delay entering this part of the ship until we could replace the missing atmosphere.

To accomplish this, we needed to trip three relays simultaneously. As Whiskers was a bit chunky, the task fell to Daniels, Heinz and myself. Each of us were in a separate Jefferies tube. I hate to admit it, but I was the last to reach my relay… and I had the other two by four decades. I was going to need to work out more.

"You guys ready," I said over the comms.

"Waiting on you, Sir," Sandy replied.

"Roger that,' Daniels answered as well.

"OK, let's do this thing," I said. "On my go, flip your relays. Three, two, one… FLIP!"

I have to admit... I was disappointed with what happened next. Nothing. Not a damn thing. No lights flickering. No distant sound of air suddenly rushing in to fill the vacuum in another area of the ship. Nothing. Just one little, completely unsatisfying, click of a relay. I know it's not much but even a 'bing' would have been better. It's the little things in life that make it worth living.

"Mitty, you old otter. We're not seeing anything happen here. Can you confirm we were successful?"

"Indeed, you were, Commodore. The atmospheric pressure in the impacted area is climbing and is already at seventy-four millibars. I would recommend allowing the level to rise to no less than eight-hundred millibars before you attempt to enter."

"Understood," I acknowledged. "Please advise when the internal pressure matches the rest of the ship. We've waited this long... we can wait a little longer to avoid even a minor explosive decompression between the various sections of the ship."

As luck would have it, the pressure in the recently repaired areas reached the ideal levels at about the same time I wiggled my way out of the Jefferies tube. I had thought it was bad going in... it was ten times worse having to push one's self backwards through the tubes. It was a good thing I wasn't claustrophobic.

Whiskers, Daniels, Lori and Mitty met me at the sealed hatch that separated the part of the ship we had been living in from the part of the ship we had just restored environmental services to.

Before I could tap in the command override on the door, Mitty stopped me.

"I must warn you Commodore. No one has entered this section of the ship since we were attacked on our way out of G.O. space. I have very limited access to the remaining sensor feeds in this area of the ship. There will most certainly be the desiccated remains of the engineering staff in there. Also, although I have a mobile emitter with me... there is a possibility that I will lose holographic coherence in this area of the ship until more repairs are done."

All of this I had anticipated and so I was ready with a plan.

"If your mobile emitter fails, we'll carry it back for you when we leave the area. If you need to, transfer to the battle bridge and use the comms to keep in touch. Our engineering optics can be used if you need to point anything out."

"Understood, Commodore," Mitty replied without even wrinkling his nose. I still didn't know that that meant. So much for my genius IQ.

Our engineering optics were a pretty nifty doohickey that Lori and Whiskers had cobbled together. They were basically old-style gas-permeable contact lens with high-resolution semiconductor nanocrystals, or quantum dot, displays built in. The *Gilboa's* AI could virtually augment what we were seeing.

***

We had covered about a third of the area... maybe sixteen rooms... when we found the first body. It looked like explosive decompression had been the cause of death.

There was no question the victim was a J'ni. Three more J'ni were found in what looked like a sealed lab.

This time it appeared that the deaths had resulted from a lack of oxygen. The survivors had managed to close the airtight door to the room, but they had no way of replacing the O2 they were breathing. In my mind, this had to be a terrible way to go. To know that death was coming and to be able to do nothing about it.

I hoped when my time came... it was something better than laying on a floor with people I cared about waiting for a death that I could not prevent or avoid.

Amazingly, we found only one more body... or at least part of one. It was right outside the hanger area that had been breached. There were char marks on the corridor wall near where the body had been found. Mitty speculated that there had been more personnel in the hanger... but that they would have been sucked into the vacuum of space... again, not a good way to go.

Sadly, that was the way of war. Plenty of ways to die... and precious few to live... unless the leaders prosecuting the war could be convinced to talk.

I think that was one of the things bothering me most about this, as yet unknown, enemy fighting the Galactic Order. The absolute refusal to communicate with anything other than a metaphorical sword meant a lot of innocent folks were going to die... had in fact, already died.

"I'm still surprised we are not finding more corpses," I said to Mitty. Whiskers was inspecting the burn marks on the wall.

"I'll take a sample of this carbon scoring on the wall for the doctor to evaluate. But you're right sonny... I mean Commodore... I can't see how all them J'ni would have been in the hanger deck. There should have been well over sixty of them and we've only accounted for what... five... maybe six of them. Doesn't add up."

"I agree with the Commander," Mitty said. "There is another possibility, but I consider it an unlikely one."

"You mean the stasis pods?" I asked.

These were pods meant to hold injured crew members in suspended animation until they could be transported to a medical facility prepared to address their injuries. In addition, ships like the *Gilboa* kept a large number of such pods onboard so as to reduce resource consumption in the event of an extended voyage.

My newly acquired knowledge of the layout of the ship told me that we were two decks above where we would find the pods in question. I wasn't willing to trust the turbo lifts. With my luck the grav-plating would continue to work fine but the safeties on the lifts would fail and I'd become the first Commodore in the history of the Federated Fleet to end his illustrious career in an elevator accident. Yet another in my ever-growing list of ways I didn't want to use to check out of this life.

Given my feeling on that matter... and because I was the boss... we used the vertical access ladders to move between decks. These were like the Jefferies tubes, but thankfully, much more spacious.

When we arrived on the deck in question... Mitty's holographic emitters flickered and went out. At the same time our comms went dead. I had no idea what was happening... and I've never been a fan of ignorance.

Lori pulled out her medical tricorder. It was one of the few pieces of Terran equipment we still carried and used. In truth, we didn't use it for its intended purpose because the GO equipment was far superior. That said, it had a large display and she carried it because it was loaded with a game called mahjong.

I used to love to play it with Lori. Sadly, it had become a boring game because I now had an eidetic memory. I still played but it was because I loved being with my wife.

In this particular instance, I was pleased that she was enamored with the game and kept the small device with her at almost all times.

The light from the screen lit the hallway. It was a strange sight. Row after row of man-sized glass tubes extended from holes in the floor. Many were dark. Some had opened, and bodies lay on the floor where they had fallen out. I could see lights flickering on some of the tubes a little further down the row.

"Follow me," I yelled.

I started jogging down the tube-lined corridor. I suddenly knew what was going on and, if I was right, we didn't have much time.

Chapter 6: Top Dog...

The stasis tubes that had lights on them were near a central hub. Status tubes branched off from that hub like spokes on a wheel.

Whiskers rushed to the main console and began evaluating the readout. He began to bark instructions to Daniels. I joined Lori at the first of the tubes that appeared to be active. There was a J'ni inside the tube and he seemed to be in distress. The creature was writhing from side to side as if it was trying to get out. There was a look of panic in its eyes that transcended species.

"We have to get them out," Lori yelled.

I grabbed the tube and tried to lift it, but it wasn't moving anytime soon. Option one was a no-show. Option two was up. I turned to Whiskers. "We need to get these stasis tubes open... yesterday if at all possible!"

"Your wish is my command," my Chief Engineer said with a grin.

Immediately the lights came up and each of the remaining active stasis tubes began to decant their occupants. At the same time Mitty flickered into existence beside me and our comms opened up.

Lori wasted no time contacting her medical support team. I did her one better and ordered all personnel to our current position to aid in recovery operations.

The J'ni that had been in the tube in front of us seemed to realize we were there to help him. Lori cradled his furry head in her lap and gently stroke his fur and whispered encouraging words.

The creature chittered something unintelligible back at her. It was obvious that he was having trouble keeping his eyes open. Whether that was from exhaustion or something far more serious I couldn't tell.

"J'ni Maktoo wishes to express his gratitude for saving his life. He wants to know how his shipmates are doing?"

"Tell him we are doing everything we can, but he should know that several... even many... did not make it," Lori said with tears in her eyes.

Mitty chittered something back at the J'ni.

The creature's eyes welled up in tears that matched my wife's. A single lightly furred paw reached up to touch her cheek where a tear had fallen. He chittered once again. It seemed more solemn this time.

Mitty turned slightly and bowed to Lori. "J'ni Maktoo is honored and blessed that you, a stranger, would share grief-water with him and his clan. You are Maktoo now."

I had no idea what that was all about but over the next few days I would learn. It turned out the J'ni had no vocal cords and so were unable to form sounds the same way we did. Fortunately, they typically wore devices that could translate their clicking and chittering sounds in the various languages used by the Galactic Order.

Some of the crew members were starting to make their way into the stasis chamber. They obviously did not share the same concerns about the turbo lifts that I had... or at least they had decided the risk was worth it given what was going on in here.

I started moving among the stasis tubes... trying to make sure none of the J'ni were missed. In the end, I was surprised to learn we saved fifty-eight of the original engineering staff.

The last stasis tube we reached held a surprise. It was a larger version of Mitty. Apparently, the crew of the *Gilboa* had included some Archons. A single living one had made it into a stasis pod. I knew that others of the political caste-race had survived the attempted genocide, but I had no idea I would meet any of them while we were still in the Sol system.

As I was helping the female Archon out of the chamber... and don't ask me how I knew she was a female... I just knew, Mitty materialized next to me.

"Is she..." The little guy's voice was strangely strained.

The Archon's eyes fluttered open and then she barked. It sounded like a sea lion. She scrambled away from me... obviously scared.

I put my hands up and backed away so as to reduce the appearance of a threat.

The female turned to Mitty and began to bark and growl in a complex pattern of sounds that were clearly a language. Mitty responded in kind and then moved towards her and wrapped his webbed paws around her in a loving embrace that could have taken place in any airport in the world.

Finally, Mitty stepped back and touched the female's head. The tips of his fingers flashed briefly. A couple of weeks ago I would have been in the dark about what was going on... but now, thanks to the Da'Tellen device I knew the Archon female had an engram transfer interface embedded just under what passed for the dura mater in her skull.

Mitty turned to look at me. The little bugger seemed to be in shock. I didn't even know an AI could be in shock. It soon became apparent as to why.

"Commodore Riker, allow me to present she who would be my wife. You would not be able to say her name, so she has agreed to go by Shella."

The larger otter looked up at me. "Well met Commodore Riker." Her voice was gentle in ways her eyes were not. I wasn't sure to be happy for my friend Mitty or not.

**

A day later, and with most of the survivors secured in the med-bay, I finally had a chance to ask Mitty for answers to the long list of questions that had been forming in my mind.

We were in the recently reopened bridge of the starship *Gilboa*. I don't know why it was... but the bridge of a starship, no matter what race built it... always seemed to look like the bridge of a starship. This one had a central seat; a big forward view screen; numerous primary consoles like navigation, sensors, weapons as well as a number of secondary ones for engineering etc. The only thing missing was a popcorn machine. More ship's bridges needed to have popcorn machines.

I tugged at the collar of my new Galactic Order uniform. It was similar, at least in color, to my old Federation uniform but rather than being multiple pieces, it was a single-piece, formfitting, lightweight jumpsuit. The reason for the change in uniform was twofold.

The new uniform was based on advanced Galactic Order tech. It could serve as an emergency survival suit with the addition of a special helmet and matching protective gloves. These items were fabricated in a way that allowed them to form an airtight seal. The uniform and the rebreather built into the headgear could keep a person alive even in a hard vacuum for a few minutes (until the power cells drained and the rebreather failed.)

The second, and perhaps more importantly, as a clone, I was no longer entitled to wear a Federation uniform. Although it pained me to admit it… my genetic progenitor was the only one with that absolute right to wear that uniform. The other human members of my crew, with the exception of my wife – who was also a clone, were either civilian contractors or retirees.

The new uniforms, which Mitty had suggested we wear, helped to establish an *esprit de corps*.

The *Gilboa's* holographic AI was at the First Officer's station. He was verifying that the ship's status displays were correctly updating as the various systems throughout the *Gilboa* were repaired. Things were beginning to move a bit faster now that Whiskers and his staff had a clue about what they were doing. I was hoping the addition of the J'ni would help speed repairs up even more.

Shella was with Mitty. The fact that she was… was a bit of a surprise given she had spent as much time in the stasis pods as the rest of the original *Gilboa* crew. She seemed to be made of sterner stuff than the J'ni.

That said, as we would learn over the many months to follow, the sole remaining living representative of her species was profoundly sad. To know that you will be the last of your kind can do that to you.

Lori had wanted to keep her in the med-bay, but the Archon would have none of it. Lori released her when Shelly had threatened to bite a nurse that had been foolish enough to get too close.

It seemed the female Archon's were the more aggressive or at least the more head-strong of the two genders. I would learn over the years that would follow that pissing off a female Archon, especially Shella, was never a good idea.

I started talking as I walked over towards the station Mitty was working at.

"So, I'm curious. With your nearly omnipresent knowledge of the goings-on on the *Gilboa*… How is it that you didn't know about the stasis pods? We could have prioritized them, if we had known they were there and were failing."

"It was and is truly regrettable. Commodore, you have to understand that I was brought online only as a part of an emergency protocol. The ship's primary AI created me from stored engrams as a means of communicating with you. I was not present during the battle that resulted in the damage that we have been repairing. The *Gilboa's* AI was unaware of the stasis tubes, and so, as a result, I too was unaware of them."

"So how long have you been… I don't even know the word to use… operational?"

"I came online six minutes after your wife was cloned. Based on conversations with her, it was decided to 'recruit' you."

I shook my head. 'Recruit' would not be the word I would use but that was old news at this point.

Shella has holding Mitty's holographic hand. The female Archon seemed upset. Still, it was obvious that the two were or had been very much in love. It was nice to know that God had allowed such niceties to transcend the vastness of space.

All that said, and as nice as it was to see Mitty with his mate, I was still getting some strong negative vibes from her. As I said before… she was upset. It could be a result of, what was for her, the recent space battle where she lost some friends… or it could be something else entirely.

"So, as I understand it, the J'ni are your engineering types. It would certainly explain why so much of the ductwork is narrow."

Mitty didn't say a word so I soldiered on. "My brain download," I tapped my head, "didn't include social dynamics. My understanding of your society is that you function very compartmentally. Humans cross-train as a matter of course. Soldiers can be medics, engineers can even be teachers. How are the J'ni going to react to working with humans who don't fit the ridged molds of your society?"

Shella stood up and walked over to me. She seemed to have a good understanding of human personal space because she encroached on mine and glared up at me. If I had to guess, I was about to learn why she was so upset. As a point of reference... there are times when I hate being right.

"Human, your questions are offensive. How the J'ni handle their affairs... is by definition... their affair."

"First, let me say that referring to me by my species is considered impolite. Second, how the crew interacts is very much my concern."

Mitty's 'better half' glared at me in a way that convinced me that Archon women were cut from the same stuff as human women. Maybe this was something universal... the thought reinforced my belief that God had a sense of humor.

"It is not your concern because it is my concern... human. I am the Archon. You are... whatever it is you are."

I could see that Shella and I were going to be butting heads if I didn't find some way to address this situation. The problem was, we humans were already committed by virtue of Galactic law. If I didn't win this power struggle, the human members of this crew... and any potential offspring, would be forced into a societal mold that we were ill-suited to live within. I had never been the type of guy that always colored within the lines and I wasn't about to start now.

Unfortunately, that forced me to put a new friend, even if he was synthetic, in an awkward position. I looked over towards the holographic projection of Mitty. I could see in his eyes that he knew what I was going to do. I hoped he'd understand.

"Mephibosheth, what is your role on this ship?" I asked even though I knew the answer.

"I am the *Gilboa's* avatar," Mitty replied.

"And, in what capacity do you serve the ship's crew."

"I function as an interface between the ship's AI and the biological crew. I am based on the engrams... the memories and experiences – if you will – of an organic sentient and thus can apply empathy to my crew interactions. In addition, I serve as your technical advisor."

"You said, 'your technical advisor'... In your capacity as the ship's avatar, do you acknowledge that I am in command of this vessel?"

"You are in command of this vessel."

"Why?"

"Because we are engaged in military operations and you are the senior military officer onboard. You have accepted a commission in the Galactic Order and are the de facto commander of record for all Galactic Order armed forces."

Now I had to slam the hammer home.

"In time of war, are warships under the command of military personnel or political personnel?" I asked.

"They are commanded by military personnel under the supervision of the overlying political structure."

"Does that political supervision include operational control of this battleship?"

"It does not."

"So, if I understand the situation correctly, Shella's role is that of an advisor… not unlike your role. Is that correct?"

"She would be a political advisor whereas I am a technical advisor… but yes, the major thrust of your statement is correct."

I think I had them where I needed them. There was just one more question I needed answered to establish the pecking order.

"Mephibosheth, if a political adviser were to attempt to command the *Gilboa* with a command that contravened an order I gave… which order would hold precedence?"

"A political advisor cannot issue an order to a ship of war during wartime."

I turned to face Shella. She was still standing right under my nose, so I was forced to look almost straight down. She wrinkled her nose. I really needed to figure out what that meant.

"Are we clear as to our respective roles now?" I asked with a firm and unyielding voice.

"Perfectly… Commodore," Shella said crisply and took a single half-step back. "My former husband has explained that you had received command engrams. You are a foreign species for which the Galactic Order has no experience.

"Forgive me if I felt the need to test them. Had you backed down in the face of a challenge to your authority you would have failed my test. We face annihilation Commodore Riker. Placing you in command of our military forces represents an enormous risk that would never even be considered were our situation not desperate. I hope you can understand my reservations. Be assured, you will have my complete support now."

She looked at Mitty and nodded briefly before turning back to me. "Given that you passed my evaluation, I am empowered and in fact required... by Galactic law... to make one command structure change."

Damn, I thought to myself. Here I thought I had won this one.

"What is this command structure change?" I said with growing concern. I decided I needed to continue to stand my ground. "If I deem it appropriate I will accept it. If I don't, then you will need to convince me why it's necessary. Fair enough?"

Shella wrinkled her nose again and stepped back so as to grab her holographic husband's hand. "Acceptable. Now we must wait."

As I was trying to figure out what we were waiting for... Lori, Whiskers and a small delegation of J'ni, including J'ni Maktoo, made their way onto the bridge. It was the first time the heart of the starship had seemed full to me. It was a nice feeling.

Lori smiled at me. Something was up. I mean don't get me wrong. I like it when pretty girls smile at me... especially this pretty girl... but none of that diminished the fact that something was going on and I was *not in the know* as it were.

Whiskers walked up to me, saluted and executed a perfect about face so he was looking back at the others.

"Attention to Orders," Commander Whiskers McGraw said in a voice that would have done any Sergeant Major proud. "Be it known that on this date, Commodore Jeremy Edward Riker is hereby promoted to the rank of Admiral of the Fleet with all the duties and responsibilities therein." Whiskers paused for a brief second and then added, "May God have mercy on his soul."

The humans in the room started clapping.

Whiskers executed another perfect about face... I was impressed. I didn't think he had it in him. He stood at attention as Lori walked over to me and removed my rank insignia. She replaced them with two sets of five stars.

I knew now what Shella had meant by a command structure change. To a certain degree I was pissed that I had been played... but I was sure I would get over it.

When the last set of stars was in place, Lori stepped back and joined Whiskers in a salute. It was funny from my perspective because the J'ni attempted to mimic the action but seemed to be unsure which arm to use.

Damn, I thought to myself. I was finally the top dog and I couldn't tell anybody back home.

Chapter 7: Dog Race...

In the weeks that followed, my newly expanded crew began to gel. I was both surprised and pleased with this as we now consisted of three distinct species: Humans, Archons, and the enigmatic J'ni.

This last group were the most unusual. As I think I shared before, they used electronic VOX devices to communicate with sentients other than their own species. In addition, they had three sexes. I don't even want to begin to know how that works.

I found out about the odd nature of their reproductive cycle because my wife had become 'Maktoo' with J'ni Maktoo. I'd love to clarify what that means but it would require my understanding what that means... and in point of fact, I'm still a little hazy on the subject despite several attempts on the part of Mitty to explain the situation to me. Let's just say... aliens are... alien... and leave it at that.

To make a long story short, my wife was invited to a reproduction ceremony hosted by J'ni Maktoo and his two significant others. Remember what I said about aliens being alien... this is what I meant.

My wife said it was a lovely ceremony and proceeded to attempt to tell me all about it. It took a while, but I was eventually successful in my efforts to convince her that there were some things I really didn't need or want to know.

About a month and a half after rescuing the J'ni, we finally got the FTL engines back online. This was good news because I was beginning to become my own worst problem. The real me had started to notice that some of the ships in the boneyard were being stripped.

The result of my former me's concerns about pirates stripping my/his boneyard was that the boneyard was now under much tighter monitoring than it had been previously. This made it ten times more difficult to secure the refined raw materials we needed to fix the *Gilboa*. I was beginning to appreciate why others thought I was such a *pain-in-the-ass* sometimes.

My wife, bless her heart, assured me that my ability to be a *pain-in-the-ass* had been a gift I had been born with and it was a part of my charm. I'm not normally a suspicious man, (ok, I am but that's beside the point), but I suspect my wife was having a laugh at my expense.

The last straw, with my former self, was when Whiskers and three of his J'ni tag-a-longs had been forced to hide for hours in a less-than-spotless commode on one of those Chinese Zǎo-Shang destroyers we had parked in orbit around Ceres.

My chief engineer swore that if he ever saw Kung Pao chicken again he would shoot the cook... and here's the deal... after seeing his face... I believed him.

I held a general staff meeting. Shella, Mitty, Lori, Whiskers and J'ni Maktoo were in attendance. The ship was about 42% operation which was hands down better than the 12% operational status we had started with.

Still, we had a way to go and I was beginning to think we needed to take some calculated risks. I had an *a priori* expectation that the Archons were not going to be fans of what I was going to suggest. What a surprise... It turned out I was right.

"You cannot proceed in this direction," Shella protested. "It violates every Galactic First Contact protocol!"

I pointed to my chest. "I think that's water already under the bridge. Your very presence in this system is a violation of that protocol."

I had done my homework before this meeting. I had anticipated a number of objections... and as my father had taught me... a problem anticipated was a problem avoided.

"Section two-one-five of the Decur Charter specifically suspends First Contact protocols in the event of imminent danger."

Shella wrinkled her nose. "That codicil was intended to apply to the nascent system only, not dangers to Galactic Order member worlds."

I passed her a tablet with a court ruling on it that refuted her claim. She scanned the tablet and tossed it on the table. I could see she was fuming... but that I had won the day. Remember what I said earlier about pissing people off by being too smart... too honest... too often? Turns out my gift extended to xenological interactions as well. I was well and truly blessed.

You have to understand, humanity was a bit of a problem for Shella's worldview. In her society, the only people who would be having a discussion like this would have been the policy deciders... in other words the Archons. The fact that humans gladly morphed into whatever role was necessary to move a project forward was deeply disturbing to her.

"Look," I said, "We will proceed with contact in a way that minimizes our exposure. We need the help and… if the Galactic Order is to have any chance of survival… we need to be flexible on the means we employ.

"If it makes you feel better, my mother always told me that rules needed to be flexible… if for no other reason than because a person's sense of ethics… right and wrong… had to be anchored and immutable. One has to flex so the other can remain firm."

"Your mother sounds like a wise person," Shella acknowledged. "I am profoundly uncomfortable with what you are proposing, but I accept that our chances of ultimately being successful would be enhanced if we… apply a modicum of flexibility. I would request one boon."

"Fire," I said.

Mitty and Shella looked around.

Lori and Whiskers started laughing.

Mitty and Shella both turned back to me and wrinkled their noses in unison. I had not seen that particular trick before.

"My apologies… I was not referring to the rapid oxidation of flammables. The term is slang for 'go ahead and ask.'"

"I see," Shella said in what seemed to be a confused voice. "If I may 'fire', I request that you limit your contact team to humans and my mate with a portable holo-emitter. In that way, you will have 'flexibility' to abort your interaction in the event the desired outcome seems unlikely."

I smiled. I had already considered who I would want to be a part of the away team. For this mission I was only planning on taking Mitty, Lori and myself.

"That's reasonable," I agreed.

I turned to my wife. "So dear, are you ready to see your dad?"

***

Admiral Spratt was not typically an easy man to see. The sole exception to his 'make an appointment' rule was his only daughter, Lori. Now technically, this didn't apply to clones of his daughter, but what he didn't know wouldn't hurt us.

We refurbished and 'borrowed' a Gnat from the large collection that the 'other me' had in orbit around Ceres.

An unfortunate string of surveillance system glitches served to hide the fact that we had absconded with the ship in question. I knew the 'other me' would be pissed, but I figured adversity helps to build character… and who doesn't want to have more character?

Gnats were fast little ships. They were designed to get in… kick the dog in the teeth… and get back out quickly. That said, there was no way we were going to fly one across the solar system. I loved my wife dearly… more so now than ever… but two months in a ten by ten-foot enclosed cockpit would seriously challenge any marriage.

Having a newly acquired top-shelf genius IQ, I decided not to do that. Instead, we flew the fully cloaked *Gilboa* to the Earth-Moon system and then launched our Gnat out of one of the working shuttle bays. This saved us about fifty-nine days out of what would otherwise have been a sixty-day journey.

The Admiral's primary office was on Hap-Ring-One of the L1 Lagrange Station, between the Earth and the moon. To avoid detection, we brought the *Gilboa* in closer to L3 which was on the other side of the moon. We burped the cloak just long enough to launch the Gnat. By the time we circled around to the Earth-facing side the *Gilboa* had moved a full quarter AU away.

Lori opened a channel to the communications center on L1. The ensign staffing the comms accepted her authentication codes and put us on, what he claimed would be, a brief hold. When ten minutes went by I began to get a little nervous.

In my mind, I could envision any number of scenarios that ended with the L1 platform's defensive array taking a pot-shot at us. I had deliberately made sure that our Gnat was unarmed and broadcasting the ident-codes for the decommissioned fighter it was. L1 might wonder why it was back in Earth space but they would have no reason to suspect it posed a threat to something as big and well-shielded as a primary Lagrange Station.

Finally, the Admiral's face appeared on the vid-screen. He was a tall man, but you couldn't tell that from the display. His once brown hair was peppered with grey. He was seventy-eight years old, but in top physical form. With mandatory retirement a decade away, he was still a very active man.

When my father-in-law saw Lori, his face lit up. It always did.

"Ordi, what a delightful surprise!"

Ordi was a pet name her family used for their daughter. I wasn't sure where it came from and no amount of coaxing had every been able to pry the secret out of any member of the Spratt family.

"Is that JD I see next to you?"

David was my middle name. As far as I knew, the Admiral was the only one to ever call me that. He never used the nickname 'Dog' or 'JD' even when everyone else in the room did. Of course, he was the Admiral, so he could call me 'chopped liver' and I would have saluted and said 'Sir, yes Sir'.

"It is… and I'm glad to see you too Dad."

The Admiral leaned closer to the screen and his eyes widened a little as he took in my uniform. Before he could say anything, I spoke.

"Admiral, I request you go to a secure channel."

"Switching over now. This better be good, son or Ceres is going to seem like a walk in the park. Wearing stars, you don't own, is a court-martial offense."

"Sir, I'm declaring an Omega-Delta event. Authentication code, Riker-captain-one-one-zed-one."

An Omega event was an imminent threat to the Federation. A Delta qualifier meant it was a game-changer… we were not alone in the universe.

The Admiral checked my voice print and authentication code. When he looked up again his face was several shades whiter.

"Lori, I can't believe I'm asking this... but please provide your authent codes," the Admiral responded with a tightly controlled voice.

"Riker-Commander-Medical-zero-niner-theta-theta-six."

"I'll be damned. You did say Omega-Delta?"

"Yes Sir. I did. It's imperative we talk immediately. Can you meet us at Lunar Two?"

"Of course, but why not here?"

"Sir, I'm asking you to trust me. What I have to share with you cannot reach the wrong ears. I'm also going to ask you to bring Colonel Jamerson if he is available, Sir."

"Negative that, son. The Colonel is on R&R. I'll bring his second, Major Morrison."

"Forgive me for asking Sir... but do you have absolute trust in the Major?"

Admiral Spratt stared intensely at me for a second before answering.

"You're really serious about this aren't you?"

"I'm afraid I am Sir. About the Major?"

"Like you son, I would trust him with my daughter."

Chapter 8: Dog Days on the Dark Side of the Moon…

Lunar Two was the first base located on the backside of the moon. It had initially been designed and built by an organization call SETI which was dedicated to looking for signals from alien worlds. Although it had detected a number of very promising signals over the years, there was never that one reproducible one that would have provided proof-positive that little green men… or talking otters as the case may be… actually existed.

My desire in meeting here was entirely predicated on the simple fact the facility was still operational… isolated and completely automated. We could meet in private.

Lori and I arrived a good hour before the Admiral and Major could arrive. I spent the time with her and Mitty discussing the possible ramifications of having the Major rather than the Colonel at the meeting. In the end, we actually considered it a bit of fortuitous luck.

Our intention was to brief Lori's dad on the entire situation and request the permanent assistance of a couple of heavy Marine platoons… maybe seventy to one-hundred Marines. A colonel would rarely be placed in command of such a small force. A major, on the other hand, would do quite nicely… if we could convince the Admiral and the Major of our need and the fact that it would be in the Federations best interest to be of assistance.

I had a secondary goal, and if I knew Lori's father as well as I thought I did… he would accommodate me.

***

Admiral Spratt, Major Morrison and a pilot who thankfully stayed on the shuttle, arrived right on schedule. Lori and I each carried a small grey box about the size of a data pad in our pockets. The devices were remote holo-emitters that would allow Mitty to appear with either one of us... even if we became separated.

I wasn't expecting trouble, but you could never tell. I still had no idea how the Admiral was going to react to his little girl being cloned. I'm sure he was going to blame me even though she was the one who got me cloned.

Once the base's landing bay had re-pressurized, the Admiral's shuttle extended a ramp and the two officers disembarked. Lori and I both saluted. The Admiral returned our salutes. I saw his eye flash over the five silver stars on my shoulder.

The grimace on his face made me rethink the wisdom of wearing my new uniform... but in the end, I realized that I was no longer a Federation officer – if given my status as a clone – I had never been one to begin with. It would be better to begin my relationship with the Admiral honestly. At least as honestly as was practical.

"This way, Admiral, Major, if you please."

I directed them to the only conference room on the small base. Mitty had previously swept it for recording devices or bugs. It was clean.

I motioned for the two officers to sit down. It looked like the Admiral was going to say something. Lori looked at him, smiled and nodded to the chair. Her father relented and sat. The major followed a moment later.

Lori and I followed suit. I took out the holo-emitter and placed it on the conference table.

"First things first," I said. "I think proper introductions are necessary. I'm Jeremy David Riker but you and I, Sir, have never met face-to-face. The original Commodore Riker was kidnapped, cloned and released with no memories of the event by an alien race representing a coalition of sentient beings called the Galactic Order. I am here on their behalf."

Admiral Spratt snorted. "You're a clone?"

"Yes, Sir, I am."

"And I'm just supposed to believe this? Are you a clone too?" the Admiral asked Lori.

"I'm so sorry, Dad... I don't even know if it's fair to call you that, but yes I'm a clone too."

The Admiral stood up angrily.

"I don't know what type of sick game you two are playing or how you talked her into it JD, but the games stop now. This has passed way beyond the realm of funny or a joke."

I tapped the little silver box.

Mitty appeared standing beside the table. Human tech could easily produce holograms but with nothing even close to approaching the fidelity of what they were seeing with the Archon.

Major Morrison stood and drew his sidearm. I ignored it. Shooting Mitty would accomplish nothing and, unless he shot Lori or I in the face, our enhanced Galactic Order uniforms would harden on the impact of a bullet protecting us.

Mitty started to speak. His deep voice was impressive. I had gotten so used to it, it wasn't startling any more. I almost laughed when I saw both the Admiral and the Major do a double-take.

"I am an artificial intelligence based on the memory engrams of a deceased member of a race known as the Archons. My organic body was murdered as part of an attempt to inflict global genocide by an unknown force attacking planets in our collective. We came to your solar system because we believe you are uniquely suited to help us in preventing additional acts of genocide."

It took a few minutes but eventually the Admiral and Major calmed down and began to listen intently to the story behind the Galactic Order's journey to find a race to aid them in their battle.

It helped that Lori suggested her pseudo-father check the transmission logs from the Ceres boneyard. A Commodore Riker had sent a validated status update less than a week ago. The best available human technology could not have gotten me to Earth in anything short of forty-five to fifty days.

Over the course of the next several hours Mitty, Lori and I laid out what had happened. Explained the damage to the *Gilboa* and the strange species-specific role casting that was apparently the norm in the rest of the galaxy.

Mitty explained why our meeting had to remain secret and our specific request for military assistance in the form of combat Marines.

The Admiral listened intently and then said he had heard enough. He would authorize a clandestine operation to assist us so long as two conditions were met. The first was that he could see the *Gilboa* first hand. We had expected this request and were prepared to accommodate the Admiral.

The second request was the one I had been waiting for all day. Lori's father demanded access to FTL technologies. I thought Mitty was going to blow a circuit breaker or something. The thing was I fully supported the Admiral's request. The Galactic Order had come into our system... after they had been attacked by an unknown force. One that had the ability to almost destroy one of the newest and most powerful of the Galactic Order's battleships.

For all the Admiral knew... that very same adversary was following a trail left by the damaged starship straight towards Earth. What chance would humanity have if such an enemy were to enter our system and use a similar bioweapon?

Access to FTL technologies would at least give humanity the ability to escape and preserve the species. Was that really too high a price to pay... given that we were helping the Galactic Order and that they were the ones to have visited this threat upon us?

In the end, I explained to Mitty once again that we could either deal with the ramifications of violating Galactic Order directives... or deal with the ramifications of no Galactic Order. The choice was his.

* * *

"Wow... look how big she is!"

This must have been the sixteenth time I had heard either the Major or the Admiral – or both at once – say the same thing... and we weren't even on board the ship yet. I couldn't wait until they got to see the tech inside the *Gilboa*... as well as an actually living Archon and of course our J'ni engineers.

The Admiral had put in a class-one secure conversation with the Earth Union President and Joint Chiefs of staff. Earth would begin a crash development program to prepare itself for a possible invasion. No one was fooling themselves into thinking we could adequately defend ourselves should the enemy invade our solar system... what we could do was get all of our eggs out of the one basket.

Lori had given her holographic projector to her father and before we left the solar system, I would make sure Earth had several of the Da'Tellen teaching machines.

I think the most interesting thing was that the Admiral had issued recall orders for the real Commodore Riker and his daughter. Apparently, he was going to follow the Archon's example and put the two of them in leadership positions for what would come to be known as Operation Diaspora.

* * *

Major Morrison wasted no time in rounding up two heavy platoons of Federation Space Marines. In the end, there were ninety-eight of the fighters and twenty-seven civilian specialists that joined the crew. These numbers included sixteen spouses that were trained in advanced sciences, engineering or medicine.

The Admiral and I had had a prolonged discussion about the inclusion of family members. In the end we agreed that it might not be in the best interest of the mission, but it was in the best interest of humanity. The one-hundred and forty or so humans onboard the *Gilboa* did not represent a great deal of biodiversity but it would likely be enough... especially given the advanced medical equipment available to us... to start a new human colony should the worst happen to Earth's solar system.

The Admiral gave me a packet of orders that I was to share once we were underway. I knew the bulk of what the packet contained. The two platoons of Marines as well as the civilian staff were being assigned to joint operations with the Galactic Order and placed under my direct command.

Second, Major Morrison was being promoted to Lieutenant Colonel. The Admiral's orders were that the newly promoted Colonel was to operate from the rear and field-promote officers as needed to prosecute the war from the front lines.

I hadn't known Morrison for long, but I expected that last order would be routinely ignored. In many ways, Morrison was just like me. I didn't know it then, but we would become life-long friends and I would be with him as he continued to rise through the ranks to the very top echelon of the Galactic Marines.

Having over two-hundred souls onboard a starship like the *Gilboa* was like having a single drop in a very large bucket... still it was a welcome change to hear the sounds of laughter and camaraderie echoing through the alien corridors. After spending so much time in the relative isolation of Ceres and the boneyard, it felt good to have people around again.

The logistics of handling the movement of supplies, work requests and a thousand other little details threatened to overwhelm me. I had felt like Moses when all the Israelites kept coming to him to adjudicate every little squabble they had. His father-in-law Jethro spoke to Moses and counseled him to appoint others to help.

I didn't have Jethro and I didn't have a host of people to help me with the administrative tasks of running a ship like the *Gilboa.* What I did have were a pair of Archons... some of the best administrators in the known galaxy. Shella had quickly taken charge and the result was nothing short of phenomenal. I hadn't realized how much faster things could progress with the right people plugged into the right tasks.

This had become a bit of a reoccurring theme. The J'ni were better engineers than my people. But Whiskers was a better man to lead the engineering staff. What made the human contingent so unique was not our ability to be superior at any given task but rather our ability to work across disciplines. We provided something the original crew of the *Gilboa*, and I suspected the Galactic Order in general, lacked. We provided a means for developing interdisciplinary synergies.

A guy named Saul of Tarsus wrote a famous letter some 2200 hundred years ago with advice to a struggling church in a place called Corinth that spoke of this very thing. I suspected it might be considered one of the oldest leadership guides still in existence. He said something along the lines of '*There is one body, but it has many parts. But all its many parts make up one body.*'

Even back then, humanity recognized the whole was greater than the sum of the parts. It made me wonder how the Galactic Order had managed to form in the first place given the lack of some unifying force. I was going to have to ask Mitty about it sometime. My musings were soon interrupted, however.

As I was walking towards the main bridge (it turns out there were three... did I mention the J'ni like to over-engineer), I heard the sound of running behind me. I turned and saw something I had never in my life ever expected to see. Whiskers was jogging down the curved corridor towards me. In a few short weeks, this ninety-eight-year-old man had gone from looking like he was in his mid-seventies to a man who might be in his early sixties.

The advanced alien rejuv tech Lori had been administering to our original somewhat geriatric crew was turning out to be a minor miracle in its own right. Mitty had said that the treatments, while effective, would be limited in their efficacy because the recipients where starting their treatments at such an advanced age. Based on what I was seeing, I don't think Whiskers was about to complain.

"Admiral!" Whiskers huffed as he finally reached me. "I'm glad I caught you. I've got some ideas I want to run by you."

"You could have used the comms. I can't have my chief engineer dying of a heart attack on me."

Whiskers snorted. "I'll have you know I've been jogging a 2K every morning for a week… Sir"

I smiled. I knew he had. I also knew the gravity plating had been set to 75% in the newly constructed gym. I knew because the Marines who, with the help of the J'ni, had built the facility in one of the many empty hanger decks, complained just this morning that somebody kept resetting the grav-plating on them. They liked to keep it at 200%.

"What's up old timer," I said as I patted him on the back. "Let's talk about it over a cup of coffee."

Chapter 9: Dirty Dog...

"The J'ni are great engineers... but they aren't innovators. You tell'm what to build and they build it. But you ask them to enhance a system and they look at ya like yer a cat in the hen house," Whiskers said.

"Can I assume you have some enhancements in mind," I asked while experimentally sipping the excellent, if somewhat excessively hot, synthetic brew.

"Ay, that I do. The main plasma conduits are leaky as a bad shower head. The J'ni keep six times as much insultation around them as they need just to protect against the radiation leakage. Every peta-watt that is absorbed by the insulation is a peta-watt that can't go to the shields or weapons systems."

I added a little cream to the cup I was sipping... I hadn't been able to adjust the temperature to that perfect point I wanted. My wife, Lori, was a master of the art, but a grown man needed to learn to pour his own coffee, and so I soldiered on. At a certain point I had more of a latte then a plain boring coffee but, at least, I could drink it without scalding my throat.

"So, it seems to me the fix would be to enhance the efficiency of the plasma conduits. If I remember the ship's schematics correctly, they're lined with some type of superconducting beryllium alloy. I would imagine a better high-temperature superconductor would do the trick," I said.

Whiskers snorted. "There ya go again... trying to teach yer grandma how to suck eggs."

"Come on Old-Timer… even a blind hog finds an acorn once and a while," I laughed. "What's it going to take to make this happen and what can we expect as a result?"

"We don't need to do all of them at once. If I can shut the primaries down for a day, the boys and I can get them taken care of. I'll get another team working on the shield emitters and weapons. They're not designed for the bigger load we'll be delivering, but I've looked them all over pretty thoroughly. I've got some tricks up my sleeve that should get'm to handle the extra juice just fine."

Whiskers took a gulp of his coffee. It was every bit as hot as mine, but decades of swigging homemade rot-gut had deadened the nerves in his throat.

"I noticed you didn't say anything about what we could expect as a return on our time investment."

Whiskers nodded.

"The shields are pretty easy to estimate. All we do with them is bring more emitters online at once. The J'ni only bring a third of them up at a time so if one gets damaged they can bring up a redundant emitter. We'll have the option of running them that way or firming up the shields by bringing more online. I imagine we'd be looking at… at least a thirty to forty present increase in shielding.

"The weapons systems are another matter. The plasma guns may not ramp up as nicely. We really won't know until we test them. The railguns on the other hand should be able to impart another thirty to forty percent in terms of kinetic energy. The downside to the kinetics is they take ejection mass. Once we shoot all of our KEWs… that's it they're done. What I'd like to do is make our KEW rounds about a third smaller… their punch would be the same, but we'd have thirty to forty percent more ammunition."

"It sounds reasonable. I'm guessing it will take a little while to refabricate the KEW ammunition. How long for the plasma turrets?"

Whiskers rubbed his chin. "I'd like ta tell ya a day but I'm probably safer saying two. We may be better off mounting additional turrets rather than putting all our time and energy into trying to reengineer the existing guns… at least until we have more experience with them."

I nodded. "Make it so Chief Engineer. You just bought yourself three more days on the schedule. Use them well."

"Aye Aye Captain"

***

It turned out that nothing is ever as easy as it should be, and the engineering team needed four extra days to get everything up and running. The *Gilboa* was still only at about eighty percent but all the major power, life support and weapons systems were operating at peek (or in some case beyond peek) efficiency.

I decided that it was time to take our leave of the Sol system and to boldly go where no man has gone before. Sadly, fate had other plans.

I was on the bridge. Whiskers was at the engineering station. Colonel Morrison was acting as my First Officer when he wasn't overseeing his Marines. Mitty was at the sensors and I had Shella running the comms. I had stolen both Daniels and Heinz from the engineering team. They were now my navigators.

I took my seat in the center of the bridge. Sadly, there still wasn't a popcorn machine but I was feeling a lot like a fictional starship captain. I decided you only live once so I decided to indulge my inner-child.

"Ahead warp factor three Number One!"

"Sir," Morrison asked in a confused – *what the heck is he doing now* – voice.

"Sorry, I just always wanted to say that," I admitted.

Sandy and John had both swiveled their chairs to look at me. Sandy had a similar look of confusion on her face. John on the other hand was smiling from ear to ear.

"Mi ween baren engines... thay canna take the strain sir!"

"As you were... Mister Scot," I laughed.

"Navigator," I said with a firmer voice. "Bring the navigational deflectors up and make best possible speed for the Oort cloud. The sooner we can get out of the sun's gravity well the sooner we can engage the skip-drive."

"Course plotted and laid in, Sir" Sandy replied crisply.

"Mister Daniels, if you would be so kind... throttle up the VASIMR drives. Adjust the gravity-plating and inertial dampeners to compensate for a sixteen g acceleration. When Commander McGraw gives you the 'all clear' push the engines to the edge. If they're going to fail, I'd prefer to know it now and not a month from now."

The 'timbre' of the Gilboa changed subtlety. I wasn't sure, but it felt wrong. I waited for Whiskers to say something from the Engineering station, but he was intent on watching his board. I decided I was imagining things. In hindsight, I wish I had gone with my gut on this one.

"Shields firming up at sixty-three percent of capacity per the flight plan," Sandy announced.

"VASIMRs are throttling up fifty percent capacity," John reported. "Acceleration ramping up along expected curves. Currently at three gravities and climbing... There are some minor variations within the forward manifold but still operating within expected norms. Twelve gravities... fourteen gravities..."

I had begun to think we were out of the woods. I should have known better. Suddenly the timbre of the ship changed drastically, and two things happened at once. The lights flickered and when out and we lost our artificial gravity. My guess was we lost thrusters at the same time which was fortunate because if the inertial dampeners had gone down while we remained under thrust... we would have been subject to a bone-crushing g-force.

"Whiskers?" I said as the emergency lights came on.

"Interesting," he replied.

"Interesting? Mister, interesting is a pretty girl on the beach. Interesting is a new beer list at the bar. Interesting is NOT when you break my pretty new starship!"

"Uh... what? Ah... yes Sir," Whiskers said in a distracted voice. "It seems there was a stress fracture in one of the fusion reactor couplings. The reactor SCRAMed like it was designed to... the secondary and tertiary reactors should have picked up the load but they SCRAMed too."

"Any theories as to why? I hate like hell for this to happen again... say... in the middle of a firefight."

Rather than answer, Whiskers got up and walked over to the sensor station Mitty was monitoring. They talked for a brief second and then both of them turned to face me.

"Sir, it would seem we have a saboteur onboard."

***

A common, but unproven, belief is that the term sabotage came from the French during the industrial revolution when striking workers would throw their wooden shoes, called Sabot, into the machinery to gum up the works. From this term we get the word, saboteur. The thought that we had somebody onboard that wanted to *gum up the works* was disturbing.

Even worse than the damage that was done... was the thought that we could not trust one another.

"Explain yourself Mister," I barked from my command chair.

"Sir," Whiskers began, "the J'ni build everything with a minimum of triple redundancy. Three separate sets of failsafe would have had to fail in order for the reactors to go through a cascade SCRAM like we just witnessed. The odds of that happening are so small as to be negligible. This was done on purpose."

"OK, let's say I believe you and it was not some random accident. Is it possible that it was an unintended result of some of the power-system modifications we have been making?"

"Ay, it's possible," Whiskers said, "but possible and probable are two very different things."

"Understood. How long do we need for repairs?"

"The damage is minor. I can swap out the coupling in thirty minutes but... I'd like some time to walk through each of the major systems. Can you give me a few hours?"

I shook my head. "You have a day and I want you to use every last minute of it... check every critical system and then check it a second time with a separate team. I want everything logged. If something else happens I want to know whose eyes were on it last."

I turned Colonel Morrison.

"Mike, you and Mitty are with me. Everybody else, I want internal sensor logs scrubbed with a fine-tooth brush. Any abnormalities I want flagged... backed up and investigated in that order. Am I clear?"

"Sir, Yes Sir"

***

"Well, this is a pisser," I said. "Maybe this is all a big mistake. Different races working together for the first time. Maybe something got missed because of innocent assumptions. Maybe there is a bit of racial bigotry going on... I mean I hope not, but that's better than a saboteur."

Mike rubbed his forehead. I had learned that was his 'tell' when he wanted to say something I wasn't sure I wanted to hear.

"Out with-it Mike. What are you thinking?"

The Marine shook his head. "You're not going to like it."

I snorted. "I already don't like it.

"What if this same saboteur was responsible for the earlier problems the *Gilboa* had leaving GO space? Mitty has admitted he wasn't brought online until after the ship entered the Sol system. How do we know the ship's computer log hasn't been tampered with to hide any earlier sabotage?"

Mitty chose that moment pipe in.

"The Colonel has a valid point. Twenty-three percent of the ship's AI core is offline and its data unrecoverable. We had assumed that the loss of this data was due to engagement with the enemy and the resulting damage that the Gilboa suffered. Perhaps this is worth investigating."

I had a bad feeling in my gut that we were about to open up a big can-of-hurt on ourselves, but I didn't see a choice.

"Mike, select two volunteers with decent computer skills. Work with Lori and get them under the hair driers – I want them to know all that they can about the *Gilboa's* computer systems and then I want them to start digging. Bring as many of the damaged cores back online and find me some answers. I also want you to assign support personnel to each of Commander McGraw's inspection teams."

I hated my gut feelings... if for no reason then they were rarely wrong. Today was no exception.

Chapter 10: Barking at Visitors…

Twenty-four hours later I was back on the bridge sitting in my customary chair. It was amazing what a difference a day could make. The sense of optimism that had accompanied our first attempt at stressing the *Gilboa* had been replaced with one, while not of dread, but of certainly less optimistic.

Our best efforts had not turned up any further critical anomalies. I wasn't sure how I felt about that. If we had found something, then, we would have known where we stood… even if we didn't like it, having a traitor in our midst. As it was, we still couldn't rule out a plain and simple accident – even given that the odds of so many interdependent systems failing at once defied reasonable probability.

"Alright, Sandy and John… let's do this thing. Bring the navigational deflectors up and throttle up the VASIMRs. Same parameters as last time."

The 'timbre' of the ship was subtly different. My gut was telling me we were OK… and for the next six days we were.

The part of the Oort cloud we were aiming for was only about 5000 AU away… still at twenty percent the speed of light, the *Gilboa* would take almost five months to get there. Fortunately, we didn't need to head out of Sol's gravity well anywhere near that far. Our actual target was just a tad over five hundred astronomical units out. An AU is the average distance between the earth and the sun. It works out to roughly eight light minutes. Doing the math, said we had about two weeks of traveling to get to where we could safely engage the Skip drive.

Our FTL drive basically warped space-time. The *Gilboa* would ride a ripple in space-time much like a surfer would ride a wave off a beach. The FLT engines could create a fold anywhere but if we were too close to a gravity well... we would be sucked into it... much like maelstrom could suck down a ship on the open sea.

The beauty of the Skip drive was that it didn't violate Einstein's pesky little rule about never exceeding the speed of light. The drive was essentially a working implementation of an Alcubierre warp drive. A theoretical physicist named Miguel Alcubierre first postulated such a drive in the late twentieth century.

The J'ni had perfected their version of the drive by developing a practical source of negative energy in the form of a massive Casimir–Polder force generator. The result was an FTL drive that could cover a light-year is as little as three days.

Not quite one week into our journey out past the orbit of Pluto we began to get some odd readings on our long-range sensors. We were seeing ripples in space-time that should not be there. Among the possibilities were a nearby collision of two massive stellar objects along the lines of super massive neutron stars or possibly black holes.

The second possibility was an approaching ship using a similar FTL drive. This was the option that had me most concerned.

Mitty had assured me that our FTL drive did not leave a trail that could be followed. That said, I reasoned, and he agreed, that a network of sensors could detect the direction and strength of a ship using a Skip drive... much like we were detecting gravity waves now. Three such sensors could pin-point a ship in 3-d space. A fourth such sensor could be used to detect the direction of movement. From that it would just be a matter of figuring out what star systems existed along the flight-path.

The Galactic Order did not have such a system in place... but that did not mean the enemy did not.

Remember my comment earlier about having gut feelings that were disturbingly accurate? I was having one right now.

Our sensors were detecting a shift in the frequency of the gravity waves we were seeing. Again, this shift could be explained by natural phenomena... it could also be explained by an FTL drive preparing to drop out of warp in the next few days.

I'm a firm believer in the age-old maxim, hard preparation – easy time; easy preparation – hard time. I began to push my people to prepare hard.

I should probably mention, I've been known to have boundary issues when I'm excited or upset or both. I think Whiskers was going to have Lori give me a sedative if I asked him one more time if his team was doing all they could. I wanted every major system running at one hundred and ten percent. I wanted spare shield emitters stockpiled as well as major components for each of the weapons systems.

I had Whiskers run two additional special jobs. I asked that he start producing KEW rounds like nobody's business. I also asked him to put a human team together to start producing fighters.

I was just as hard on Colonel Morrison. The fighters were for him.

The *Gilboa* had massive hanger bays. Surprisingly, they were completely devoid of fighter aircraft. Mitty had explained that when the Saulites were wiped out, there simply were no fighter pilots to be had. The Galactic Order had three member-races that could fight but without military leaders to set strategy the battle loses had been staggering.

Fortunately, the onboard fabrication systems were able to convert boneyard scraps into serviceable combat aircraft. The designs were modified because humans tended to be larger than most of the other races that were part of the Galactic Order. Also, some of the components needed to make the original designs where beyond the abilities of the *Gilboa's* fabrication systems to reproduce. If the task had been left up to the J'ni, that would have been the end of it. Human ingenuity, however, filled in the gaps.

Morrison had had his men training on simulators. If the gravity wakes we were seeing turned out to be invaders, the *Gilboa* would be the first line of defense.

We were about a light-day out from Earth. That made real-time conversations impossible. Instead, I put together periodic data packets with log entries, system reports and a complete set of sensor data. Hopefully Admiral Spratt would do everything he could to beef up the Federation's defenses. If the enemy was coming... if they were already here... these might well be Earth's last hours.

Two days later our worst fears were realized. I brought the *Gilboa* to yellow alert. Four starships, each somewhat smaller in size than the *Gilboa,* emerged from Skip drive warp bubbles. Their relative speed was about fifteen percent light speed and they were on a vector that would take them further into the Sol system.

Based on the data we were able to glean from the collapsing warp bubbles it seemed that their combined mass exceeded our own. The fact that there were four of them meant that we would have to face four discrete adversaries as opposed to one. Unfortunately, that meant they could bracket us. Assuming, of course, they were hostiles.

To my way of thinking, we only had two advantages should it come to a fight. First, our weapons likely had a longer reach—although there was no guarantee that this was indeed the case. Second, we were a hell of a lot meaner... and that was most certainly the case.

"Helm, vector us to intercept. Shed our forward velocity if you need to. And Sandy, use the cold thrusters. We've got plenty of time to make these course corrections. No sense advertising we're out here."

"Aye, Aye Admiral."

"Mitty, bring up the forward viewscreen. As soon as we come within visual range, I want to see what we're dealing with."

The holographic Archon acknowledged my request. We were still several hours from being able to see them. It wasn't that they were too far away for the *Gilboa's* optical sensors to detect them... it was simply that it would take that long for the light from their point of emergence to reach us.

Now I know what some of you are thinking... How did we know four spaceships emerged from FTL? The answer is simple, gravity waves riding on top of warped space-time travel faster than light. That means we could detect the interlopers long before they could detect us. I planned to use that to our advantage.

We had already reached our cruising velocity of 0.2 the speed of light. The ships that had just entered our system were much closer to the Oort cloud than we were. Their approach vector put them no closer than two astronomical units from us.

I had the *Gilboa* ramp her newly enhanced shields up to full power. This would effectively hide us from passive scans. I was betting these new ships would not utilize aggressive active scans until they were much further in system. Any sensor data they pulled back now would be days old by the time they received it.

I ran the math in my head... which, when you think about it... was pretty remarkable, in and of itself. I had been a low one-forties genius before this adventure had started, but even at that, a year ago, there was no way I could have pulled off what I was doing now. Thanks to the Galactic Order teaching machines I now had one of the highest IQs in Federation space.

Our two sets of ships were traveling at a little under a third of the speed of light relative to each other. Without changing the Gilboa's speed, even with revectoring, we would only be in weapons range of the alien vessels for a few seconds. This was OK if the aliens were friendlies but what were the odds of that?

I used a quick Fourier transform to evaluate the gravity waveform that we had recorded from each of the unknown ship's warp-bubble emission signature. That gave me what I needed to calculate the mass of each of the other ships. When I crunched the numbers in my head, I quickly confirmed the each of the four ships were essentially the same size.

I checked what I now knew about the interlopers against the available data in the *Gilboa's* library. The enemy that had attacked both the Archon and the Saulite homeworlds used ships of roughly the same mass and sublight speed.

It wasn't absolute proof that we were dealing with the same folks... but if it looks like a pig, smells like a pig and oinks like a pig... there's a damn good chance you can make bacon out of it.

Given their velocity, I now had a pretty good idea how much energy they would need to revector away from a pursuing *Gilboa*. Their mass to power ratio would need to be considerable higher than ours in order to escape us... should they attempt to flee. The question was... would they?

This was my problem. If they were the bad guys... (and I was reasonably confident they weren't just stopping by for tea and crumpets), and they chose to flee... then we would need our current speed to chase them. On the other hand, if they chose to slow down and slug it out… then we would need to shed our speed as well.

"Mike, Mitty… with me in my ready room."

***

"Look JD, I get what you're saying but the bottom line is, we have good reason to believe that we have a significant edge in our power to mass ratio," Mike said. "We can accelerate faster. That has to be the deciding factor."

In my ready room I encouraged a certain sense of informality… names rather than ranks… that sort of thing. I found it promoted a better brainstorming session.

We had been weighing the pros and cons of our next actions for the better part of twenty minutes. My concern had been, and continued to be, how close were we going to let these guys get to Earth and the inhabited colonies on Luna, Mars and the Asteroid belt?

If I made the wrong choice… our theoretical greater acceleration would allow us to turn and catch up to the four alien ships, but not until they were almost within striking range of our most vulnerable population centers.

It was a classic damned if you do and damned if you don't. My father had always taught me to go for option three when faced with something like this. The only problem was I didn't know what option three was in this case.

"Mike, I'm inclined to agree you," I sighed. "But I want to look at this thing from all angles. We have the luxury of time to contemplate our next move. God isn't always so generous."

I took a sip of my coffee. I'd gotten the temperature right this time. I added some cream anyway.

"It seems to me… either way we go could end up being the wrong choice. I'd rather make the wrong choice having weighted all the options… than make the wrong choice because we didn't weigh all the options."

I turned to face the other 'person' in the room.

"Mitty, you've been very quiet," I said. "The purpose of a meeting like this is to bang ideas back and forth. Care to share your thoughts?"

The holographic otter, sat straighter in his seat and waved his hand towards the conference table. As if by magic a second holographic image seemed to flow out of his fingers and grow to fill the space above the table.

I might have mentioned in passing before that my inner geek was seriously in love with Galactic Order tech. It was crap like this that got my juices flowing… I'm sure Mitty could have just sent a command to the ship's computer to have the new hologram appear above the table… but where was the fun in that? No… he added the finger-flowy thing. It's the little touches that make all the difference in tech. I was glad the Archons and the Galactic Order appreciated such subtleties.

I realized my mind had wandered and I looked at the hologram Mitty had summoned. It appeared to be a ship. Its configuration looked nothing like the *Gilboa*. To be honest, it looked more like something a human would build… although a heck of a lot bigger and complex.

"This is a representation of the raiders that have been attacking GO worlds. Its mass seems to be consistent with what we are detecting in the four ships that have entered the Sol system. If they are indeed the same type of ship… and if they have not been modified from the ships we have experience with… then we know they can accelerate faster than we can but have a significantly lower top operation speed because of their shielding. That means in close-in fighting they have an advantage but in a long chase the *Gilboa* would have the advantage."

I nodded. We knew all this. Mitty knew that we knew so he must have some other point.

"Since we cannot know how they will respond to us… we cannot know whether we should maintain speed of begin deceleration. The logical choice would be to…"

"Do both," I finished for him.

Mitty wrinkled his nose. Whether that was from irritation that I had cut him off in my excitement… or if he was pleased that I agreed with his reasoning… I couldn't tell.

Mike looked at the two of us.

"Somebody want to let us mere mortals know what you're thinking?" Mike said with just a little irritation in his voice.

Chapter 11: Dog Fight...

I looked at Mitty. "You want to do it, or shall I?"

"It's your ship, Admiral."

I shook my head in defeat. The Archon had never really gotten into the spirit of the whole 'informal' thing. Mike and I had tried on several occasions to get him to loosen up. The closest we had gotten him to being informal was to call me Admiral Dog and the big Marine... Colonel Mike.

I leaned over table and grabbed a virtual representation of the *Gilboa*. I guided it along the table towards the ship Mitty had just added to the display.

"Here's what we're thinking. We slow just enough to match their velocity and revector to more closely match their course. We do all of this just prior to reaching weapons range. That way if they choose the run option... we are in a good position to pursue. Meanwhile, well outside of weapons range, we'll launch a full flight of fighters.

"The fighters, which are faster and far more maneuverable, will intercept the intruders and keep them busy should the aliens choose the hard deceleration option. That will give us time to slow and return to engage our four friends."

"It makes sense," Mike said. "But what happens if they go for option A and decide to slug-it-out rather than decelerating? My guys are stuck in the middle of nowhere with no ride home."

I shook my head.

"Got ya covered buddy. These aren't like your grandpappy's fighters. The new toys your guys will be flying can do about twenty-six gravities... maybe a little more. Even with the inertial dampeners, it won't be a picnic... but it should be more than enough to get you to the *Gilboa*."

* * *

Not long after, we broke up the meeting. We still had a little while before we came into visual range. I decided to grab a quick bite from the mess.

Lori joined me, and we talked about little things. Neither one of us wanted to discuss the possibility of an upcoming firefight inside the Sol system.

We had both caught the tail end of the last Federation dust-up but neither one of us had been in command of anything at the time. I had been a shuttle pilot and she had been a medical intern.

My grand contribution to the war effort had amounted to nothing more than dumb luck. I had been in the right place... at the right time. A bunch of fighter jockeys that had gotten their ships shot out from under them. I simply used the shuttle I was piloting to make a detour. The fact that the detour was into an active combat arena and that shuttles aren't known for speed or shielding were side issues in my mind. They contributed to the risk that I took... but it was a personal risk. The shuttle was hit about sixteen times but by the grace of God the engines kept working.

People had said that I had been brave and fearless – I'm not so sure. A great general from a bygone era, George S. Patton once said:

If we take the generally accepted definition of bravery as a quality which knows no fear, I have never seen a brave man. All men are frightened. The more intelligent they are, the more they are frightened.

I was frightened then and I was frightened now, but for entirely different reasons.

I was frightened now, not for myself but for the men and women I might have to put in harm's way. It didn't matter that every one of them was a volunteer. This time around, I would be the man that sent them. I suspected that I would emerge from the other side of this a changed man. It turns out I was right. On a side note, I hate it when I'm right about crap like this.

***

"We are in optical range," Mitty announced. "Bringing up the enhanced image of the main view screen."

The four white dots that we saw suddenly resolved into slightly larger images. The resolution at this distance was not good but even I could see that the ships in question looked very much like the raiders that Mitty had shown Colonel Morrison and I in the Ready Room.

"Crap." Mike muttered softly from someplace behind me.

I shared his sentiment. I mean, I knew intellectually that the odds of these ships being something else was astronomically low, but hope is a part of the human condition and we are at our best when we refuse to relinquish it.

"Bring the ship to red alert," I said calmly. "Lieutenant Daniels, ahead flank speed until we catch up with them."

We had spent the last several hours carefully revectoring ourselves using a cold ion thrust. Unfortunately, we had a lot of momentum carrying us in the wrong direction. We were going to have to shed that momentum by accelerating hard in the opposite direction. The engine's exhaust would be pointed away from the ships we were approaching and the bulk of the *Gilboa* would also help to hide the hot ion gas, but no one was fooling themselves into thinking we would not be noticed.

The good news was it would take the radiation signature from our VASIMR drive several hours to reach the other ship by which time we would be well on our way towards catching up to them.

"Lieutenant Heinz, refine our course per what we discussed earlier. Bring us on a parallel course just outside of their weapons range. If they turn in any direction… don't wait for my order. Adjust to remain just outside of their bite."

"Roger that, Sir"

For the next few hours, we played a game of cat and mouse. Contrary to classic science fiction like you might see on a holovid, space battles were long drawn out affairs. Finally, when we got to within 0.6 A.U. of the enemy raiders, we received confirmation of their intent.

All four of the ships we were pursuing began to fire grape-shot from their lateral rail-guns. The idea of the grape-shot was a simple one. If we continued to accelerate into these small bits of fast-moving metal, we would be adding our kinetic energy to theirs and amplifying their deleterious effect on our shields. While our shields were still recovering, the enemy would likely fire their energy weapons.

The only problem was I had anticipated this possible plan of attack. Call me a spoil-sport, but I wasn't inclined to play their game by their rules.

"Colonel Morrison, be so kind as to let your men know that they are a go in approximately five minutes. Then if you would, deliver our surprise package."

Our surprise package was a new weapons system just installed on the *Gilboa*. Typically, our railguns fired a single kinetic round or grape-shot like our mysterious enemy had. The modifications we made to the *Gilboa* allowed her guns to launch special carrier shells that encased small fusion missiles with their own VASIMR drives. The weapons could achieve three times the top-rated speed of the Gilboa.

That meant we could use the explosion of the nuclear payload to clear the grape-shot out of our path long before we were in range to be affected by the blast. In addition, the EMP should seriously confuse and blind any active sensors... at least, that was the hope. Our own sensors were timed to briefly deactivate as the detonation took place.

I felt the *Gilboa* shudder as two of our surprise packages left the tubes at near relativistic speeds. The energy used to launch them was impressive... especially given that it was enough to shake a ship the size of the *Gilboa*.

"Hyper-velocity missiles away, Admiral. Course is good. Missile two is vectoring 2 degrees to left as per plan."

"Very good, Colonel Morr..."

Before I could finish the two devices detonated. The flight deviation between the two missiles was enough that the one did not destroy the other before it could detonate.

"LAUNCH FIGHTERS!" Morrison barked.

The intensity of the nuclear flash was beginning to fade enough that the bridge viewscreen, which had turned opaque, was once again displaying the field of engagement.

The four enemy ships were starting to spread apart, and they sought to surround us. It looked like they were going to take the running fire-fight option... at least that's what I thought in the beginning. The reality is, in war, no plan ever survives contact with the enemy.

"One of the ships is accelerating slightly. Its course has been adjusted as well. Recalculating its trajectory," Sandy said as she worked her board. I had a bad feeling I knew what she was going to say next.

The Lieutenant looked up at the forward viewscreen and then turned to me.

"Sir, its Earth. They're heading to Earth."

Sometimes, I truly hated being right. This was one of those times. The enemy knew that we had greater acceleration. The three ships staying behind forced our hand. If we pursued the one speeding ahead, we'd have to deal with the other three closer to our inhabited worlds. On the other hand, if we engaged these three, the fourth would have an uncontested shot at humanity's homeworld.

Earth had defenses... the question had to be – would they be enough to defeat a threat of this magnitude?

"Send a secure packet to Earth," I said. "Send a copy of our logs and advise them we are engaging three of the ships. Number four is going to be theirs to handle."

I turned to Mike. The Marine had set his jaw and had a grim look on his face. I knew from the intensity in his eyes that what I was about to ask... he had already resigned himself to do.

"Colonel, we need to stop that last ship. Whatever it takes."

"I understand, Sir."

"If you would prefer, I can give the order."

"Negative that, Sir. They are my men. I need to be the one to give the order."

I nodded. The Colonel spoke quietly over the ship-to-ship comms. He was ordering his fighters to chase down and engage the fourth alien ship. It would be like bees stinging an elephant. It might irritate the elephant but it sure as hell was not going to stop it.

Even worse, it virtually guaranteed none of the fighters would have the fuel to return to the Gilboa. If they didn't manage to stop the fourth ship, the Gilboa would have to give chase... assuming she survived her engagement with the other three. In any case, the chances were good that the air supply on the fighters would run out before we could come back for them.

In essence, we were sending forty men and women to their deaths.

I watched helplessly as twenty of the most advanced fighters ever to fly in the Sol system rapidly accelerated to engage an unknown enemy in what would likely be their first and only sortie.

The bridge fell into a silence as each of us said a prayer for the brave Marines who were about to give their last full measure.

"Three minutes to weapons range," Mitty announced from the sensors station. His words broke the solemn trance that had enveloped the *Gilboa's* bridge.

"Shields to one hundred and ten percent. Bring all plasma turrets to bear on the nearest bogey. Rail-guns are to load HVMs and launch a full spread at the other two ships. Let's see if we can't keep them occupied while we deal with the first one."

***

The battle started off well enough. I was thankful that Whisker's tweaks had enhanced both our shields and our weapons. We hit the first of the enemy ships with sixteen plasma beams, each about five percent more powerful than the ten we had started with.

In about ten seconds their shields buckled, and we began taking big chucks out of their hull. Suddenly, they stopped maneuvering. It looked like we had killed their power systems. We needed intel and I wanted prisoners, so I ordered my gunnery teams to start working over one of the other ships.

The two remaining enemies began a hard acceleration along the lines of the one that was already headed towards earth... only their vector was wrong. I was pondering what that meant when the first ship we had attacked, exploded.

The blast was orders of magnitude stronger than I had ever experienced. Mitty told me later that the enemy's ships always self-destructed, and they used some type of antimatter scuttling charge. The *Gilboa* was engulfed in the blast.

There was no doubt in my mind that our enhancements just saved our lives. That said, I was going to have to have a conversation with my holographic friend about sharing critical information in a timely fashion. After-the-fact was not my idea of timely.

Fortunately, the shields held just long enough… but then they failed. We lost almost a foot of ablative armor in a fraction of a second. Powerful x-rays bathed the ship. Half the crew was going to have to start radiation treatments after this was all done.

The inertial dampeners tried to compensate as the ship was literally knocked thru space like a billiard ball on a pool table. Panels sparked, and a thin haze filled the bridge. The dampeners helped, but crewmembers were still tossed across the bridge and elsewhere on the ship.

Colonel Morrison went flying over the railing and would have been seriously hurt had someone not broken his fall… that someone was me.

Chapter 12: Wounded Dog

With my shoulder dislocated, I crawled back to my command chair.

"Status report," I barked.

"Minor damage on decks three and four," Mitty reported. "No hull breaches but the aft shield emitters are simply gone. If we take a hit anywhere near that area we are going to be in serious trouble."

"Rotate the ship. Keep our damaged side away from those two other ships," I groaned.

My arm hung useless at my side. I used my good hand to tuck the bad one into my shirt. It hurt like hell but that was the best I could do to immobilize it at the moment. I was sure the medical staff had much bigger concerns than a dislocated shoulder.

There wasn't a question in my mind that those enemy ships would try a flanking maneuver to hit our weak side.

"Pay attention Helm. Keep our shields out."

"I'm trying, Sir," Daniels said. "She's just not responding like she should."

I could tell he was hurting too. It looked like a broken arm. His face was a mass for sweat. I had to give him points for grit.

"Mitty, Daniels needs to get to medical. Can you take over navigation autonomously?"

"Affirmative Admiral," the hologram said.

"Sir, I'm good. I can stay at my station," the Lieutenant objected.

"I know you can Lieutenant but in ten minutes the Doc can have that bone fused and I won't have to worry about you passing out. Get a move on and get back here as fast as you can."

"Roger that, Sir," Daniels said as he made his way to the lift.

"Admiral," Mitty interrupted. "I'm having trouble with computer control. It seems to be blocking my attempts to keep the damaged shields out of the direct line of fire."

As he said this the *Gilboa* shuddered. Plasma beams struck near enough to the damaged section that some of their energy leaked through. If we didn't get a handle on things soon we were going to be toast.

"Weapons, load rear-facing railguns with heavies. Fire when ready."

"Sir," Colonel Morrison said. "There's no target back there."

"Just do it Mike. Mitty, when he fires, disable station-keeping thrusters. There should be enough rotation vector to turn the ship."

We ended up playing a cat and mouse game for the next few minutes. The big break came when we managed to catch one of the two ships with a cloaked nuke that we floated in space along with some debris we had collected. If the bad guys had taken a good look; they would have seen some very *un-Galactic Order-like* Gnats floating among the debris. The Gnats were cloaked and held our little nuclear surprises.

When the nuke took out the second ship, it also self-destructed. We were ready for it this time and had put more distance between us and the resulting antimatter blast. I had the Colonel queue up and then launch three more HVMs at the last ship right as we detected the blast from bogey two.

In a few seconds, bogey three joined one and two. For the first time since the battle began, we could stop to take a breath. It was a ragged breath and we would start the chase again soon enough. Such was the way with war.

Daniels was back at this post. Sandy had a massive bruise on her forehead. Besides my arm, those were the only injuries on the bridge. Neither Engineering nor environment had been as lucky. Casualties reports were coming in all across the ship. Lori was going to be busy for a while.

I decided to tough it out a while longer with my arm. There were others that were having a much harder go of it. In hindsight, that may not have been the finest example of my newly enhanced cognitive abilities. It just goes to show that even the smartest of us can be stupid.

"Helm, best speed. Let's head on over to our boys taking on bogey four."

I turned towards Colonel Morrison and grimaced as I tugged my arm. I was beginning to wonder if it might be more than just a dislocation. I gritted my teeth. That was a problem for another time.

"Mike, what's the word?"

The big man shook his head. I could see in his eyes that it was not good. Sadly, I was not surprised.

"We're down to five effectives. Some of the other fifteen might have ejected but there's a lot of hard radiation floating around out there. It looks like they acquitted themselves well… bogey four paid a heavy price for my men's blood. The enemy ship is still on course for Earth, but her acceleration curves are way down. We should have no problem catching her just shy of Mars' orbit. And then I will take great pleasure sending them back to the hell that spawned them!"

I nodded in agreement.

"Give the recall order. Let's get the SARs ready to deploy and let Lori have a shot at saving the survivors."

***

In the end, of the forty men and women sent out to take on bogey four, only six survived. The total butcher's bill for the entire engagement was sixty-four souls. Eight of them were J'ni caught in a Jefferies tube that collapsed. The rest were homo sapiens. The entire rescue operation took about forty minutes. This was only possible because each Marine had a biotag embedded in their shoulder that facilitated locating them.

The entire time we searched and recovered our fallen and surviving Marines I fretted about that fourth ship heading towards Earth. Both Mitty and Morrison assured me we had plenty of time to intercept them, but I was nervous none-the-less. That and my shoulder and arm were on fire. I would need to do something about it soon, but I didn't feel I could leave the bridge. Instead I opted for a mild analgesic and a stim. My command chair was able to administer both.

The *Gilboa* was in bad shape as well. Her drives were still working at close to full efficiency but about a third of the ship was open to the vacuum of space and/or too radioactive to enter without protective gear. More concerning, we had lost two thirds of her weapons and a significant amount of both active and ablative shielding.

What that meant was that we had to be careful with our own acceleration curves. As we headed towards the inner system we would pass an area where the solar wind exactly balanced the pull of gravity on a cloud of micrometeorites. The cloud formed a shell around the sun. The density was actually quite low… less than a few per cubic kilometer.

That may not sound like much but, given such a huge volume of space as well as the distance and speed we were traveling, even a micrometeorite a fraction the size of a kid's marble would pack a hell of a punch.

As soon as we finished our SARs operation, I issued a series of orders. We would accelerate at our best possible speed until we reached the danger zone. Since we had to keep our best shielding facing forward, we'd kill our acceleration and reorient the ship as we plowed through this narrow band of space within our solar system.

It was a bitter pill to swallow. It meant the sole remaining enemy ship was going to get a heck of a lot closer to Earth than I would have liked. It was getting harder and harder to think straight because of my arm. It had gone from a persistent ache to a full-blown fire. There was too much to do, and the stakes were too high. The shoulder and arm were going to have to wait.

I tried to get Whiskers and his crew working on the shielding, but after several 'give me a minutes' he had finally confessed, there just wasn't much he could do. The surface where the shielding was missing was one big slagged mess. There simply were no shield emitters left to repair. The only solution was to send out repair droids to install new emitters and the power conduits to feed them.

This would have been an ideal solution except that most of the repair droids were in a section of the ship that had been destroyed. This in turn meant that the Engineering staff would need to fabricate new droids before they could undertake the shield repairs.

I was about to order Whiskers to prioritize the shield repairs over every other system when I suddenly started to have a hard time breathing. I tried to get up out of my command chair, but I didn't make it. My world started going black.

Maybe it was my enhanced intellect or maybe it was just my being a stubborn cuss... but I was pissed that I had not been able to give that final order. My last memory was seeing the bridge turn sideways as I rolled onto the floor instead.

***

"He's coming around."

Man, I loved waking up to that voice. It was my Lori. Some of my neural circuits must have still been jumbled. I couldn't figure out *how and why* my wife was on the bridge. We had a boat load of sick and injured. Why wasn't she in the Med-Bay? I still hadn't opened my eyes yet. I was waiting for the ship to stop spinning.

"You should be taking care of the injured…" I managed to croak out. *What was wrong with my voice*?

"If you weren't one of those injured I'd be hitting you right now," Lori said with a venom that caused me to crack open my eyes. Yeah that was a mistake. It was much too bright.

"Computer, dim lights 50%," Lori ordered.

"Go ahead and open your eyes, Admiral."

That's how I knew I was really in trouble. Lori never called me by my rank unless she was ticked off for some reason. I searched my, admittedly foggy, mind to remember what I had done to give offense. I couldn't think of anything off the top of my head, but that didn't mean much. Guys had been pissing off women for thousands of years without ever being able to figure out why.

"You're mad," I said as I cautiously opened both eyes.

Rather than say anything, Lori shined a pen-light into each eye. It felt like somebody stabbing needles into my head. Why did doctors always insist on hurting their patients? I tried to push the light away, but I realized my arm was encased in a plasta-cast.

"Well, your pupils are both responding normally. I'd say you managed to avoid giving yourself a stroke… this time."

I tried to sit up but failed miserably. It seemed I was in the Med-Bay after all.

"Stoke? From a dislocated shoulder?" I said in disbelief.

"You stupid... lovable... but stupid fool. Your arm was fractured in three places. Bone marrow traveled to your lungs and caused a pulmonary embolism. You could have died."

"Well, that would explain the pain," I said glibly. "As far as dying... that was never going to happen."

Lori put her fists on her lovely waist and stared at me. It seemed she wanted me to explain myself. Given a total lack of common sense and undoubtedly no small amount of pain-killers flowing through my veins... I did the worst possible thing a man in my position could. I answered her.

"I'm too busy to die," I said resolutely.

She spun on her heals and spoke to the two Marines that were standing at the foot of the bed.

"Get him out of here before I kill him myself. And Admiral..."

There it went... I was in trouble again.

"If you ever pull a stunt like that again, I'll let you die and then take great pleasure in kicking your cold dead corpse."

Here's the thing you have to understand about Lori and me. We both have tempers. I had no doubt she meant every word she just uttered... including the ones under her breath. That wouldn't stop her from pulling my bacon out of the fire... nor would it stop her and I from making up later in a more intimate setting. And when I say *making up*... well... nuff said.

Chapter 13: Dog Bite

Finally, back on the bridge, I had to admit my shoulder and arm felt a lot better. Lori had used a bone fuser and encased everything in a medicinal plastic that would both immobilize my arm and slowly infuse medicinal enzymes, steroids and topical analgesics for the next several days.

I was physically exhausted and would have gladly slept for the next week but there was no time. I had been out for almost three days. Apparently, the pulmonary embolism had seriously compromised the amount of oxygen my body, and specifically my brain, received. Lori had used some of the advanced Galactic Order medical tech to reverse the damage that had been done.

If I had still been at my post on Ceres, there is little doubt I would have died or suffered permanent brain damage. That was a sobering thought. I guess, in hindsight, I understood why Lori was pissed. Fortunately, I hadn't died and the crew of the *Gilboa* carried on without me.

It turns out, Whiskers had anticipated my last, un-issued order. His team of engineers had twenty-five percent of the shields restored in the areas that had been burnt away by the first bogey's antimatter blast.

They had worked overtime to get dozens of repair drones fabricated and deployed. My near-death experience seems to have motivated the crew to go the extra mile. I have to admit, I was surprised. I hadn't thought that I had had enough time to form that type of bond with the crew.

Whiskers explained it to me years later. What I had failed to appreciate was that every time I rolled up my sleeves and cleaned a filter or replaced a burned out and/or fused component... what I was really doing was building and solidifying a reputation with the crew. I was an Admiral and yet I wasn't above honest work.

I suspect it was my defective upbringing. Whenever I saw something that needed doing, and I was free and, in a position, to do it... I did. You'd be surprised how many odd-looks you could get as an Admiral sweeping a floor in the mess hall, so the cook would have the time to bake those special chocolate chip cookies you enjoyed.

The bottom line was the crew had accomplished a week's worth of repairs, underway no less, in about three days. It was impressive by any measure.

We were about twenty million kilometers behind the final enemy ship. We still expected to catch up with them just inside the orbit of Mars. The good news was that meant we would be close to one hundred million miles from Earth before we engaged the enemy. The bad news was, at the speeds we were traveling, the Federation defense force would not be a factor in stopping bad guys. Human tech just couldn't travel at these speeds... at least not yet.

If we got lucky, the Earth fleet might get a few shots off as the fourth bogey passed them halfway between Earth and Mars. The defensive platforms in Earth orbit and the moon were non-factors.

Even if they managed to take out the enemy ship... the antimatter scuttling charge would make the asteroid that formed the Yucatan peninsula some sixty-six million years ago seem like a ping-pong ball. And that was the best-case scenario. If bogey-four simply crashed into Earth... given that it was still traveling at a substantial fraction of the speed of light… well… it would be *Bedtime-for-Bonzo*. The Earth, and all life on it, would die.

I needed some type of force multiplier. Something that would give us a better chance of defeating this foe before they could take out Earth. A seemingly unrelated call from Engineering proved to be just the answer I needed.

"Admiral, McGraw here. Can I run a thought by ya for a minute or two?"

I flicked the comm-button on my command chair. It was still awkward having to use one hand for everything, but I was getting used to it. A holographic display of my chief engineer floated in front of me.

"What's up Whiskers? Did you get the rest of those shields up yet?"

"Aaaa, I got me boys making droids as fast as we can. We're not going to get ya much past thirty percent and that's iffy. No, I wanted to talk with ya about the weapons systems. Every forward plasma turret is toast. I can mount one or two external systems, but they'll be as delicate as a debutant at her first ball. I was thinking maybe we could do something else."

"Ok, I'll bite. What are you thinking?"

"So, our HVMs were a real hit at the last party. Only thing is, the guest of honor had his own going away surprise. We ended up getting pretty badly busted up because we were too close to the action as it were."

I looked at the cast on my broken arm and nodded.

"That we were. What are you thinking... develop a hyper-velocity missile with a longer range?"

"Aye, that would be nice but it's a tradeoff between how much mass our railguns can fire and how much fuel we stick in our missiles. The reality is... we are already at pretty close to the prefect balance now for the size of our railguns... and before you ask... there's not a lot we can do outside of a drydock to enhance our railguns."

"OK," I said. "I presume you called to talk to me about more than *what we can't do*."

"That I did Admiral. I want to fire our missiles slower."

***

Exactly one day and four hours later, Whiskers delivered on his promise. Our HVMs originally fired from our railguns. In point of fact, that was still our primary weapon. Now however, thanks to the engineering wizardry of the J'ni under the leadership of Commander McGraw, the *Gilboa* now sported seventeen externally mounted racks of twenty-each HVMs.

Rather than launching with our railguns and then using chemical thrusters for the last little push... our new missile racks relied exclusively on their chemical thrusters. Each missile was capable of accelerating to about forty thousand kilometers per hour. This was nothing compared to the existing velocity of the *Gilboa*, but it was many times the closure rate between the *Gilboa* and the enemy ship.

The problem was that chemical thrust would be like big flashlights in the dark... telling the enemy exactly where to shoot.

That's where the genius of Whisker's plan came in.

"Weapons, are all racks ready for release?"

"Confirmed, Sir. Racks one through seventeen are armed and ready for deployment."

"Excellent. I'm assuming the Engineering team has our little surprises ready in each of the railgun tubes."

"Commander McGraw confirms they are primed and ready to fire Admiral."

I turned to face Mitty. The holographic Archon looked like a huge otter fascinated with the forward viewscreen. Mitty turned his head in my direction and blinked. I knew he was nothing more than an AI driven hologram, but it was hard to watch him and not think he was flesh and blood.

"You ready to take control and make this happen?" I asked.

"Affirmative Admiral. On your command, I will release the external racks and use lateral thrusters to gently push them away from the ship. Since they already have our current velocity they will essentially match our course and speed. When the proper separation is reached I will fire railguns one and four... followed three-point-eight seconds later by railguns two and three.

"The HVMs are programmed to diverge from each other in flight. As we are three light-seconds out, I will instruct each warhead to detonate its nuclear payload when it detects the proper separation from both the *Gilboa* and its nearest neighbor.

"One second before the detonation I will instruct all three-hundred and forty external missiles to fire. The nuclear blasts from the HVMs will cover the exhaust plumes from the slower missiles. By the time the HVMs have done their work, the primaries will be on target and have gone cold. Given their stealth nature, they will be almost impossible to detect."

"Very good. Make it so number one," I said in my best British accent.

"Sir?"

"Fire, Mitty, Fire."

* * *

Everything went off like clockwork. If bogey four had any clue what we were doing, he gave no indication.

Twenty-seven minutes later we were almost in striking range. The enemy had dropped several nuclear mines. They'd have been serious trouble if we hadn't spotted them first. Our point defense lasers took them out before they got anywhere close to us.

Whiskers had actually gotten our forward shields up to thirty-eight percent, exceeding his estimate but still grossly understrength.

Our slow missiles cruised by the enemy ship without making a sound... not that you could hear in the vacuum of space... but you get my point.

I watched the countdown clock move towards zero. It seemed to take forever. All those holovids of dramatic space battles with ships whizzing past one another... don't believe the hype. It never works that way. Space battles are long periods of 'wait' followed by short bursts of 'holy crap... what just hit us.'

We were down to half a light second of separation. It was time to get to work.

"Light'm up Mike. I want a full spread of HVMs and every plasma toaster we have left firing. I want that ship so focused on us... they never see what hits them from the other side."

I felt the *Gilboa* shudder as her massive railguns fired. Moments after the railguns had done their thing, the ship rotated to bring her remaining plasma turrets and shields to bear.

"The enemy is returning fire and deploying countermeasures," Shella reported from the sensor station that Mitty's Archon wife had volunteered to man.

I this case, counter measures included chaff that greatly reduced the efficacy of our plasma beams. Our HVMs were taken out with point defense lasers before their chemical thrusters had finished their acceleration. I had had a feeling the enemy would adapt to our attack based on our last encounter. I was OK with that because I still had a trick or two up my sleeve.

"Colonel, if you would be so kind as to launch round two."

The *Gilboa* shuddered again. This time three HVMs where launched and one purely kinetic missile. My expectation was that the enemy, whoever the hell they were, would take out the first three and miss the one trailing behind because it had no thrust plume.

"Mitty, trigger phase two."

At about the same time as I gave the order to begin the next part of the attack, we began taking hits from enemy missiles. Had our shields been fully operational I don't think we would have even felt the blasts. As it was, I had to fight to stay in my chair. With only one arm it was a struggle. As silly as it sounds, at the time I was more concerned about what Lori would do to me if I re-broke the arm then I was my own safety.

"Rotate the shields," I yelled. "Do we have any point defense systems still online?"

"Negative Admiral," Mitty replied. The AI wasn't even mimicking actuating control systems. The central computer was directly interfacing with the ship's systems trying to stay ahead of a series of cascading failures. Thankfully, Mitty's last radio command to the stealth missile fleet was successfully transmitted.

On the far side of the enemy ship, hundreds of heretofore hidden nuclear missiles fired minute retro thrusters.

Bogey four most certainly saw them but there was little he could do. The one disadvantage to traveling at the types of velocities we were… was that it was physically impossible to make a significant course change.

Their plight was made worse when the last missile from our second round exploded a mere five kilometers behind them. The nuclear fireball engulfed the rear of their ship. The radiation alone would have caused serious issues for any of their crew in the compartments near the engines.

At roughly the same time explosion after explosion occurred in front of the ship. Although these blasts were further away, the sheer number of them and the energy they released, would shred the bogey's shields.

This is it, I thought. *We have them.*

How wrong I was...

Chapter 14: Broken Dog

It seemed whoever was in charge of the last enemy ship, was intent on carrying out their mission, even if it meant their own death. While I had expected them to self-destruct like the other enemy ships had done... I had assumed it would be in the form a massive antimatter explosion.

It was not.

Moments after the last of our stealth nukes had gone off... the fourth enemy ship disintegrated. Any other time this would have been a cause for celebration. The ship had shattered into pieces as large as a bus to as small as an office stapler. Each and every one was traveling at near relativistic speeds. Every one of them was on a direct course for the Earth-Moon system... and there wasn't a damn thing I could do to stop it. In four days the Earth would become the latest casualty in a war we didn't start and barely understood.

***

I had spent the morning on the horn with Admiral Spratt. Lori's father looked even more haggard than I felt. The Earth Defense Force which was tasked with maintaining the peace in and around the Earth, as well as the Federation, had deployed as many ships as they could. We all knew it would not be enough... not by a long shot.

Development of the advanced tech that the Galactic Order had provided had barely gotten off the ground. Sadly, given a few years, systems based on the knowledge provided could have easily defended against such an attack.

The Earth's best defense remained the *Gilboa*, but my ship was only being held together with duct tape and a whole lot of praying.

The ideal solution would be another antimatter bomb to vaporize what was left of bogey four. Sadly, there had only been four in system and they all belonged to the bad guys. The *Gilboa's* computer library had the specs for what was called a zero-point bomb.

The mechanism was easy to build, but to generate enough material to make a big enough boom was going to be an issue given the amount of time we had. The closer we got to Earth, the more of the vaporized bad guy would hit the atmosphere.

Conversely, the farther away we were the higher the probability most of the enemy debris could be deflected from hitting the Earth.

Vaporizing the bad guy was not a perfect answer. It wouldn't be as bad as actually hitting the planet with a solid bit of bad guy the size of a bus… but stripping away half the atmosphere was bad enough.

"What can we do to make this go faster?" I asked for the umpteenth time.

The answer was always the same. Not a damn thing. The engineering team was working as fast as they could and if they made even the tiniest mistake, the *Gilboa* would go up in the brightest explosion ever seen anywhere near earth.

Given that we could wake-up dead any moment, I decided we needed to pursue other options. We had a stockpile of roughly six thousand nuclear warheads… apparently the

Galactic Order folks liked to collect them. It was a good thing that they did, because as it turned out, our zero-point bomb didn't get completed until days after the debris entered the Earth-Moon system.

The nukes really wouldn't do the job as far as vaporizing the stuff heading towards Earth, but it might be possible to push the lion's share of it out of the direct path of the planet. I had Mitty set up an around the clock schedule for blowing nukes up in front of the debris cloud. At the same time, I recommended that all lunar and LaGrange stations be evacuated.

Pretty much anything in Earth orbit on the side that took the hit was going to be toast. If we couldn't deflect enough mass, Earth was fix'n to step back into the dark ages... and that's if she got very lucky.

To say there was a panic on my homeworld was an understatement. Everything that was space-worthy or could be made space-worthy was loaded and flying. Riots ensued as the lower classes, without the means to escape the coming apocalypse, began to seize the last remaining transports. There was a complete and utter breakdown of society.

Even if the worst of the coming threat was dealt with... humanity on the planet Earth would never be the same. I didn't know it at the time, but that was a good thing. Sometimes adversity raises up leaders that might not have otherwise shined brightly enough to be seen. A nobody, from the backwoods of Kentucky, named Robert Kimbridge was just such a man.

Twelve hours out from Earth, we finally ran out of nukes. Admittedly, the last several hours of our days-long effort would not serious affect the outcome. We were simply too close to Earth at this point.

The good news, if there was any, was that the bulk of the relativistic debris from bogey four had been deflected away from Earth itself. Oh, don't get me wrong, they were still going to get a royal pasting, but it would not be nearly as bad as it could have been.

The moon was not so lucky. At 14:53 Greenwich time in the year 2151, three large pieces of bogey four impacted Earth's only natural satellite. A full three percent of the moon's mass was ejected into space. Much of it would fall back to the moon but sizeable pieces would remain in orbit for several centuries... creating a minor ring around the planet.

Earth wasn't massive enough for the tidal forces exerted on the lunar fragments to form a permanent ring. Instead, the pieces would either float out into space, fall back into the moon or crash into the Earth as lunar asteroids.

I suppose it might be beneficial for me to explain, briefly, what happened to my homeworld in the aftermath of the attack.

A German philosopher named Friedrich Nietzsche once said, '*That which does not kill us, makes us stronger.*'

The *Bogey Four Event*, as it came to be called, would be a seminal turning point for humanity. The realization that there were threats out there in the deep dark of space, that dwarfed the petty squabbles that we had amongst ourselves, proved to be a powerful motivation for planetary unification. As I said before, in the face of adversity, some men rise to the occasion and become powerful leaders. They were the very embodiment of Nietzsche's declaration.

Earth wasn't killed by the destruction that rained down on her that day, but it had been close. Many died and would continue to die as the world struggled to put itself back together.

The majority of the larger strikes hit open water. At the speeds the debris was traveling, even objects no bigger than a baseball could flash vaporize tens of thousands of gallons of water.

Tsunamis ravaged every coastal city on the planet. In some cases, entire countries simply ceased to exist. Tens of millions died in the flooding alone. Those coastal cities that did survive found themselves without electricity or basic services.

From a power and infrastructure point of view, the United States, Europe and Africa fared the best. Each of these areas no longer used power grids for energy distribution. Instead they relied on small, local liquid thorium power generation systems. South America and the Russian Republics did not fare as well. Oligarchies, with vested interests in maintaining the *status quo*, stood in the way of many innovations. Their people paid a deep price for their leaders' short-sightedness.

The *Bogey Four Event* meant the mean temperature of the oceans rose by four tenths of a degree Celsius. That doesn't sound like much, but Methyl hydroxides, long buried on the ocean floor near the coastlines, began bubbling up... dumping thousands of metric tons of methane into the atmosphere.

Methane is twenty times as powerful as carbon dioxide as a greenhouse gas. The result could have been a run-away thermal event that would have made the mass-extinction of the dinosaurs look tame.

Fortunately, two factors came into play that saved Earth. First, enough dust and debris were kicked up into the atmosphere, especially by those strikes that occurred on land, that the planet actually experienced an extended period of cooling. Second, we now had access to Galactic Order terraforming technology. That technology would now become a lifeline for saving us.

In some ways, we got very lucky. The major industrial centers were not heavily damaged. In addition, the Federation shipyards were on the far side of the planet when the Earth-Strike occurred. This allowed the most critical recovery efforts to proceed quickly.

My father-in-law, Admiral Spratt issued emergency orders prioritizing repairs to the *Gilboa*. In short order, over two thousand technicians were crawling over her hull... repairing damage and enhancing systems as they went.

Most of these technicians had received Da'Tellen training. The work on the *Gilboa* would be good practical experience for them. One the *Gilboa* was fully operational, a new united Earth would begin a crash program to develop her own starships. The first vessels would be small, especially compared to the massive *Gilboa* but Earth would never allow herself to be defenseless again.

Three months after the attack on Earth, the Gilboa was once again ready to venture forth. We had taken the opportunity to make a number of enhancements. The J'ni were beside themselves with the changes but once you gave them a set of schematics they could follow, they settled right down.

We decided that we would invite twenty of the J'ni to stay on Earth and help with the integration of Galactic Order technology with human fabrication limitations. I was sad to see J'ni Maktoo volunteer along with his spouses. I had grown accustomed to the Racoon-like critter.

I couldn't understand a word he said without a translation device... but he liked coffee so that made him aces in my book.

In exchange for the J'ni, we got two more companies of Marines as well as replacements for the ones that had died in battle. I made sure that the families of the men and women lost knew, in no uncertain terms, that they had bought the Earth's survival with their sacrifice. I presided over the unveiling of the Gilboa Seven. A memorial that honored the fourteen Marines, in seven fighters, that valiantly took on a ship a thousand times their size... and secured victory for us.

The six survivors each received a promotion two grades above their current rank. In addition, they were offered full retirement with benefits or a chance to remain on active duty and take command of one of the sixteen new squadrons being established on the Gilboa. To a man (or woman) they chose to stay on active duty. I was told by one of them that there was a debt owed. We still had no idea who the enemy was but there would be a reckoning when we met them again.

* * *

Admiral Spratt and I spent a lot of time together as the *Gilboa* was being repaired. There was a lot to talk about. I even got to meet my doppelganger. I have to admit, seeing a man who was in every way my twin was a bit unnerving. The whole name issue became problematic. We started referring to each other by rank... and then the Admiralty board screwed that up.

The newly promoted Admiral Jeremy Riker – the original – was heading up something called Operation Diaspora. The idea was to get some of humanity out of the nest and into the stars. This way, even if Earth was destroyed... the human race would survive. In many ways, I envied my *brother from an actual mother*. He was going to get to be an explorer. I was relegated to becoming a warrior.

It took a few weeks to get things moving on Earth again. The Admiralty Board had seized effective control of Earth via a general declaration of Martial law. The old power structures recognized that a divided Earth was not up to the task of defending itself from an Interstellar threat.

There were those rulers that wanted a unified world government with them as the head. The aforementioned Oligarchs were a prime example. The masses quickly quelled that movement. They remembered being left high and dry in the days before the Bogey Four Event.

My orders and objectives were clear. Earth needed to know who our new enemy was. We needed to know what motivated their attacks... and we needed to know how to stop them.

While I was now an officer in the Galactic Order, I was also a human being. This presented me with a potential conflict in priorities. I spoke with Mitty and Shella about the problem. Mitty's wife assured me that like all males – regardless of the species in question—I was being foolish.

In her role as Ambassador, Shella met with Admiralty board and recommended the United Earth Alliance establish formal diplomatic relations with the Galactic Order. In this way, the interests of Earth would be co-equal with the interests of the Galactic Order. In short, we would defend each other and my role as Admiral of the Fleet for the Galactic Order would mean I also had a responsibility to protect the interests of my home planet.

Chapter 15: To Boldly Go Where No Dog Has Gone Before…

"Admiral on the bridge!" My new First Officer yelled as I stepped out of the turbo lift.

"As you were," I said. Ever since the crew compliment of the *Gilboa* had tripled, things had gotten more formal. I missed the causal shifts where the only people on the bridge were personal acquaintances.

My new First Officer was a woman named Commander Elena Shelby. She seemed to be of mixed Indian and African descent.

I knew immediately that she was going to be a problem. Not because she wasn't an excellent officer… she was. Her problem was she was an exotic beauty. This wasn't her fault and to be honest, there wasn't a man alive who would ever complain. One look at her tended to have those of us that could grow beards dropping our jaws.

Don't think for a moment that Lori failed to notice the reaction of every male on the bridge including a certain Admiral that was already spoken for. I think it tainted her view of my new First Officer. It would be several months before the ice sheet between them would thaw… all it took was a near death experience and a single bottle of beer… but that's a story for later.

The problem with Shelby was her perception that others didn't take her seriously because of her attractiveness… or that her rapid rise through the ranks was a result of her looks and not her God-given abilities. Actually, neither was the case. Admiral Spratt had assigned her to the *Gilboa* because she was the best candidate for the job.

Because Shelby questioned whether people respected her abilities, she compensated by being a by-the-book, tough as nails stickler for the rules, taskmaster… both for herself and for those in her command.

My problem was that a First Officer is intended to be my interface with the crew. If they were terrified of her, she could not perform that function. The whole affair was complicated by the fact that, as you may have noticed, I'm not a by-the-book type of guy.

I decided to handle the situation by setting an example that would be hard to ignore. Two technicians followed me onto the bridge.

I pointed to a space between the sensor console and the Ambassador's observation station. It was a small, recessed, alcove that functioned as a micro-galley. It could provide water, coffee, tea and various food bars for those times when it was impractical to leave the bridge.

"Install the new equipment there, men. Make sure its locked down tight. It's not the type of thing we want flying through the bridge should we get in a firefight again."

As I expected, Commander Shelby walked over to my command chair.

"Begging the Admiral's pardon. I wasn't aware of any additional systems to be installed on the bridge."

"Not to worry, Commander. It's a mission critical piece of equipment that's being installed per my personal orders... and with the expressed approval of the Admiralty board."

"Very good, Sir," Shelby said with just a hint of curiosity in her voice.

I actuated the bridge log recorder on my command chair. Admiral Spratt had made me promise to record her reaction when she realized what was being installed. She did not disappoint.

Fifteen minutes later I was enjoying a fresh bag of popcorn.

***

Aside from a few trivialities, like a popcorn machine, the *Gilboa* received a number of significant upgrades. She was no longer even in the same class as the broken and damaged ship that had crawled into the Sol system almost a year ago. It seemed, given the same basic knowledge, that humans were far more adept at innovation than many (if not most) of the other members of the Galactic Order.

The twenty-one J'ni that remained on the ship held the human engineering staff in almost religious awe. I began to wonder if the aliens were going to begin to think of themselves as second-class engineers. The thing was, they weren't. Not by a long-shot. The little buggers were far more adept at detecting and diagnosing a problem then humans were.

It wasn't at all unusual to see one of them stop in the middle of the hall... place a hand on the deck plating or a wall and then go scampering off to fix some doohickey three decks away. It was almost like they communed with the great ship at a spiritual level.

Still, it became obvious that there were the beginnings of a cultural rift developing between the humans and the J'ni. A rift, that if left unmanaged, threaten the efficiency of ship operations.

I sat down with Shelby and Whiskers to discuss the issue. After several cups of coffee and a half-sipped tea we hit upon a possible solution.   It turns out Shelby didn't like coffee—what can I say? God still loves sinners.

Maybe it was her bringing a female perspective into the mix... or maybe it was the strange way her mind worked – not liking coffee and all—but it was my new First Officer that came up with the winning solution. Let the J'ni own, lock-stock-and-barrel, those things they were uniquely suited to handle. Recognize their contributions and affirm their value to the crew and mission.

Frankly, I've never been a touchy-feely type of guy. My way of motivating the troops usually involved a boot and a subsequent visit to the proctologist. Lori had suggested I develop my interpersonal skills. She might have a point. For all I knew a solid kick to the behind might be the start to a courtship ritual with the J'ni... I was still having nightmares about the *reproduction ceremony* Lori had been invited to attend.

Suffice it to say, I left the touchy-feely stuff to those emotionally equipped to handle it.

I had Shelby draft orders awarding Meritorious Service awards to each of the remaining J'ni. These service pins doubled as universal translators that could understand the J'ni chitter.

The Raccoon-like members of the crew were given the choice of wearing their VOX devices or the new Service medals. To a man... or whichever of the three sexes they were... they chose to wear the medals.

I also promoted the J'ni named Sa'Mi to Lieutenant Commander. This gave Sa'Mi the same rank as McGraw – although the J'ni had less time in grade. Sa'Mi was placed in charge of the twenty other J'ni. Their primarily responsibilities included ship diagnostics, maintenance and repair. Both officers were to report to senior staff meetings. For the purpose of the chain of command, Sa'Mi was to appoint a second and was himself to report to the Chief Engineer which was a post currently held by Whiskers.

**

Our journey towards the Oort Belt was far less eventful this time around. I eagerly awaited the chance to experience Skip Drive FTL travel for the first time... *To boldly go where no man had gone before*... as it were. It turns out that wasn't technically accurate, but I didn't know that at the time.

It took the better part of five weeks to get to our preferred jump point. I had the crew go over the ship one last time. I was still concerned about several anomalous events that had occurred in the midst of battle. The facts said they were the result of a damaged ship being pushed beyond its limits. My gut told me it was something more.

Finally, the day we had all been waiting for arrived. We were at the jump point. We were far enough from any gravity wells that our drive could safely warp space-time and create what was essentially a ripple in the fabric of space that we could ride like a surfer rides a wave.

To me, it would have made more sense to call the damn thing the Surf Drive, but hey I don't get to make these types of decisions. Mitty assured me that Skip was a more accurate translation of the J'ni term for the drive. Who was I to argue with the over-sized racoons?

I had invited Lori to the bridge. I wanted her by my side as we made this historic leap into the world of interstellar spaceflight.

"Number One, take us to 0.3 lightspeed."

"Aye Admiral," Shelby replied crisply.

"Helm, confirm shields are at full strength. Throttle up VASIMRs to one hundred and ten percent. Ready Skip Drive," Shelby ordered.

"Shields at full strength and stable Ma'am," Lieutenant Heinz confirmed.

"Sublight drives have throttled up to one hundred and ten percent. They have quite a bit more to give if you'd like to try them out Ma'am, Admiral," Daniels added.

Shelby looked at me. I nodded. It made more sense to try out our enhancements in friendly territory than in the middle of a war zone.

"Very good Lieutenant. I understand you and Commander McGraw have discussed the engine and power enhancements at great length. In your estimation, what is a safe maximum load on our VASIMRs?"

"We should be able to push three hundred percent of the original rated capacity easily. The shields and inertial dampeners are rated at well past that."

Shelby smiled… something that was exceedingly rare while she was on the bridge. She was stunningly gorgeous when she did that. As Lori was staring right at me with dagger eyes I pretended not to notice.

"Throttle up to two-fifty. No sense pushing the engines too hard until we've had a chance to kick the tires a few times."

"Aye, ma'am. Two-fifty it is," Lieutenant Daniels said with just a hint of disappointment in his voice.

I could understand the Lieutenant's feelings. It was tough to have a new sports car and not want to push the pedal to the metal to see what it actually had under the hood. What impressed me most was that the sounds and slight tremors in the ship that I had associated with pushing the engines near capacity were completely absent.

The engineers at the space dock had worked miracles. I don't know what the enemy had in their arsenal to throw at us, but one thing was for sure… the next time we met up with them, they would be in for one hell of a surprise.

"Approaching 0.3 light speed," Sandy announced not ten minutes later. I was impressed.

"Throttle sublights down to ten percent as we reach the target velocity," the First Officer ordered.

It was a funny thing about relativistic speeds. You normally think of space as being one large vacuum. But even a third of the way towards the Oort cloud there were still stray molecules of hydrogen and what-not floating about. To a ship the size of the *Gilboa*, traveling at the speeds she was, it was like trying to run while chest-deep in water. Thus, the need to continue engine thrust just to maintain speed.

I turned to our resident FTL expert.

"Mitty, are we a go for Skip Drive activation?"

The Archon hologram used his hand to toss up three virtual displays in front of his console.

"The Skip Drive is online. The dark matter collectors are fully charged. The compression field shows we have obtained sufficient forward velocity."

"So," I prompted, "are we a go for Skip Drive?"

The Otter-like Archon looked at me and did that nose wrinkle thing that he does.

"Yes, Sir. We are a... 'go'"

"Hot diggity Dog!" I said.

I toggled the inner-ship comms.

"Attention crew of the starship *Gilboa*. This is Admiral Riker. We are about to engage the Skip Drive. For most of us, this will be the first time traveling at FTL speeds. We have no idea what the effect will feel like. We may not even be aware of the transition to Skip Space. This will be the first time this drive system has been used in well over a year. The ship has been through a lot since then. We have done everything that can be done to ensure the drive will work correctly.

"That said, there is always the chance of the unexpected rearing its ugly head. I need each and every one of you watching every board, every relay, every power coupling like a hawk. If something bad is going to happen... I want to know about it before it happens. The J'ni are our best assets in this part of the operation. Take your cues from them.

"That is all... and welcome to the new frontier. Admiral Riker out."

I looked over at Lori. She was, as always, beautiful. Her uniform hugged her body in all the right places. Have I mentioned before that she has a lot of 'all the right places?' I wondered why men's minds always seemed to drift to towards the erotic when we were about to tread where angels fear to walk. A smile must have crept onto my face. *Down Boy*, I thought to myself.

Lori must have misunderstood why I was smiling. She indicated a small box in her right hand. *Good*, I thought. Tradition dictated that we would need that box in a few minutes.

"Helm, you are clear to engage the Skip Drive at your discretion. Course as plotted before. Make it so."

"Engaging Slip Drive now," Sandy said as she pushed a double bar handle forward at her station.

There was a thrumming sound that I could feel in the base of my teeth. It wasn't quite unpleasant, but it was on the verge of getting there. Fortunately, it only lasted a fraction of a second.

"We have successfully entered Skip Space," Mitty announced. He stared to say something more, but I did not hear it. The sound of cheering on the bridge was too loud.

Chapter 16: A Dog's Guide to the Galaxy...

On July 20th, 1969 a couple of men named Neil Armstrong and Buzz Aldrin landed on the moon. It was the first-time humanity had stepped onto the surface of something with a substantial gravity that was not the Earth.

What most people are unaware of is what transpired shortly after their lunar module touched down on the moon's surface. This is a matter of historical fact and has inspired explorers in the centuries to follow.

Like many scientists, Aldrin was a man of deep and abiding faith. It seemed the more we knew... the more we knew... we didn't know. The idea of a master planner... an uncreated Creator, while abhorrent to some, was profoundly appealing to others.

Aldrin was a Christian. He asked his Pastor, a Presbyterian minister named Dean Woodruff, to consecrate a small vial of wine and a piece of bread. After the lunar module had landed safely on the moon, Buzz Aldrin said these words over the radio. They have been etched in my memory since I first attended the Space Academy.

> *"I would like to request a few moments of silence ... and to invite each person listening in, wherever and whomever they may be, to pause for a moment and contemplate the events of the past few hours, and to give thanks in his or her own way."*

During that moment of silence, he took out the consecrated wine and bread and read from a three-by-five card words first attributed to Jesus.

"I am the vine, you are the branches. Whoever remains in me, and I in him, will bear much fruit; for you can do nothing without me."

What Aldrin did has become a sort of ritual within the Space Corps. The first person to land on Phobos, a moon of Mars, did the same thing. The same was true of Ceres and if rumor has it correct, the poor souls that crash landed in a failed attempt to be the first to walk on the surface of Mars had planned to do it.

To my knowledge, we were the first humans to enter Skip Space. It seemed to be the perfect time to honor tradition... and maybe say thanks to the Big Guy.

The *Gilboa* had a chapel. What was interesting was that we – meaning the humans onboard the ship – had not built it. It seems a connection with the divine was not limited to humanity. I still wasn't completely sure I believed in all this religious stuff... but I did believe in luck and in tradition – within reason.

The box Lori carried contained a small flask of wine and a piece of unleavened matzah. They had been consecrated in the chapel by one of the new engineers, a guy named Kirkland, who was also an ordained minister. The long and the short of it was that continued what had become a long-standing tradition. It felt good to be a part of something bigger than myself.

***

Our stay in Skip Space lasted about four hours this time. According to Mitty, traveling on artificially induced space-time waves was something akin to throwing pebbles in a large pond. The ripples where the rock entered would spread out in all directions but would also peter out over time and distance.

There was also the problem of gravity wells in the middle of our flight path. Running into one of them would be most unpleasant. I asked Mitty what happened to you if you were to run into a large gravity well. He was brutally honest. He didn't know because no one had ever returned from such a misadventure.

Perhaps the most startling revelation about Skip Space was the fact that once you entered it… you did not fall out of it until the wave attenuated on its own. To control how far you travelled, you had to adjust the size of the Space-Time perturbation you created to enter the Skip-Stream.

What this meant in practical terms was it was far better to take a handful of small jumps then one large one. Now, a four hour jump only moved us to the far side of the Oort cloud. About half way to Alpha Centauri… just a tad over a half a parsec for those that are keeping track. Maybe one point six lightyears give or take a few feet.

My point was we had dropped a very small pebble in the space-time pond. In the grand scheme of things, a four-hour jump was almost absurdly small. That said, I intended to make about ten more of them.

I had two reasons for wanting to do this. First, this whole Skip-Drive thing was pretty new to us hairless apes. We didn't know what we didn't know. A series of small jumps would be just the thing to give us the experience we needed.

The second reason was because the last time somebody had made a big Skip into our little corner of the galaxy Earth almost ended up biting the big one. The enemy apparently had some type of long range sensor net that could detect ripples in Space-Time. Keeping our jumps short... at least in the beginning meant we could hide our point of origin.

The other thing we did was to shift the approach vector to our ultimate destination. By the time we got ready to make "normal" jumps, we were a good twenty lightyears away from Earth.

Our next five jumps would bring us to the edge of what had been Galactic Order space. Each of these jumps would take about a week. Our destination was an open cluster of stars called the Beehive Cluster or sometimes the Praesepe Cluster. It consisted of some one thousand plus stars, a good third of which were similar to Earth's Sol. The size was something on the order of twelve parsecs.

The intriguing thing about the star cluster was that half of all its mass was within twenty-four lightyears of each other. Earth's nearest neighbor was over four light years away. In the Beehive nearest neighbors were often spitting distance away.

This had serious ramifications for the alien life that lived in this cluster. Most races had been aware for thousands of years that they were not alone in the galaxy. Earth, on the other hand always suspected they were not alone but until a broken and desperate *Gilboa* had stumbled into our solar system, we had no definitive proof.

***

By day twenty we had made three big jumps. I was feeling good that things were going smoothly. After each jump we continued at sublight speeds for about a day to check over each of the ship's systems careful. I still had a nagging feeling that something was amiss.

At one point during our battle with the four bogies in the Sol system both Whiskers and Mitty had been convinced we had a saboteur onboard. Despite an exhaustive search, we had never been able to find definitive proof. That said, we were still plagued by the occasional, unexplained glitch.

Mike shared my concerns. He, fortunately, had something he could do about it. The Colonel ran his Marines hard twelve hours a day, six days a week. His reasoning extended beyond simply making sure his people were prepped for action. A tired Marine stayed out of trouble. A bored Marine was the very definition of trouble.

I was on the bridge shortly after having breakfast with Lori and Shella. It seemed the Archon enjoyed human food, especially eggs over easy.

"Sir, I have inbound contacts. Sixteen of them," Ensign Rodrigues reported from the sensor station.

"Yellow alert!" I barked. Toggling my comms I called Commander Shelby to the bridge. She had just gotten off duty and was likely trying to get some rack time, but I knew she would never forgive me if we had an alien encounter and I didn't call her to the bridge.

I was about to call for Mitty, when, as if by magic the holographic Archon materialized beside my command chair. I nodded to him and then turned to face forward.

"Ensign, put the best visual you can get onto the main viewscreen."

The sixteen ships seemed to be roughly identical in size and shape. No human would design a ship that looked like them. They were rounded rectangles with odd looking appendages hanging off at every angle. They were clearly not designed for atmospheric operations.

I turned to Mitty. "Analysis?"

"They are Tas Talons, Admiral. The Tas are quadrupeds that are essentially peaceful unless provoked. They are not a member state of the Galactic Order, but we have enjoyed peaceful relations since our first survey ships encountered them six-hundred of your years ago."

"Is it normal for them to send sixteen ships out to greet visitors?"

Mitty shook his head in a very human gesture. "I have no record of them ever sending out more than two. The Talon fighter…"

"FIGHTERS!" I yelled. "Those are fighters coming at us?"

"Affirmative. The Talon fighter was designed for cargo transport escort. They carry a low yield plasma turret and two ship-buster missiles each."

"Ok, that doesn't sound too bad. How dangerous are these 'ship-buster' missiles they're carrying? How big a bang do they make?"

"The missiles in question do not carry explosives. They are tipped with neutronium, an extremely dense neutron-degenerate form of matter. They are designed to punch a hole in the side of the ships they are attacking."

I looked at the little otter. "Can they hurt us?"

"Most definitely. I would recommend avoiding engagement with the Tas."

"I thought you said they were peaceful. What are they doing with neutronium-tipped missiles?"

Mitty turned to look at the screen again. "They believe in peace through strength," he answered. "It is curious that they are in this system. It is a long way from their territory."

Commander Shelby arrived while I was talking with Mitty. She was dressed in civilian attire... a Sari if I was not mistaken. She obviously decided that stopping to change into her uniform was time she could not afford. I was glad Lori was not on the bridge. The commander's attire was... well... distracting... let me just leave it at... *I was glad Lori was not on the bridge*.

"Was there a change to the uniform-of-the-day that I'm not aware of Commander?" I was joking of course. My First Officer was as by-the-book as they came.

"Negative, Sir," she answered crisply. "I was on a," she paused as if considering her words, "on a date, Sir. I heard the yellow alert and per my understanding of section 3.1.6 of the ship's standing orders I came directly to my duty station."

"I see... section 3.1.6 you say?"

"Yes, Sir."

I was tempted to pursue the matter further... if for no other reason than to discover who her helpless target was... but I had thirty-two ship-buster missiles to think about.

"Commander, tie-in the ship's universal translator and try to hail our Tas friends out there. Assure them our mission is peaceful. We meant no offense and have no interest in contesting this system."

"Hailing the ships now. No response."

"Mitty, any chance the Tas are the unknown enemy we have been fighting?"

"Highly unlikely Admiral. The Tas are a mining culture. Their ships and infrastructure are all geared to that purpose. They are one of the oldest... if not the oldest civilization in the sector."

At that moment Colonel Morrison arrived on the bridge. I was somewhat surprised that it took him this long to get here. He too was in civilian attire. Based on the quick look he and Commander Shelby shared, I suspected I knew who the hapless victim had been. The poor Marine never had a chance.

"Number One, try hailing them one more time. This time warn them off or we will defend ourselves."

I swiveled my command chair to address the Colonel.

"Mike, I want a plasma beam ready to fire. One percent power level. If I give the order fire a shot across the lead ship's bow. Let's see if that doesn't get their attention."

"Sir, there are two ports opening up on each of the ships. They could be weapon's ports," Lieutenant Daniels said. He attempted to enhance the resolution and managed to zoom the display slightly on the ports in question.

"Mitty?"

"Confirmed, Admiral. They are weapons ports."

"Mike, let them know we are serious. Commander Shelby continue to attempt to hail them."

"Roger, Sir," the two echoed as one.

A bright blue plasma beam flashed out from the *Gilboa*. There was no reaction from the advancing ships.

"Shelby, patch me into the ship-to-ship comms."

"You are ready to go, Sir."

I straightened in my seat.

"Attention Tas fighters approaching my position. I am Admiral Riker of the Galactic Order Battleship *Gilboa*. We mean you no harm, but we will aggressively defend ourselves. Please close your weapon ports and cease your advance on our position."

I turned towards Shelby. I did mention I was glad Lori wasn't on the bridge?

"Any reaction?"

"Yes Sir. They have accelerated," she reported.

"Mitty, I need answers. Why would a supposedly peaceful race be hell-bent on attacking us?"

"Unknown, Admiral. I have asked Shella to join us. She may have insights that I lack."

No sooner had he said the words then the lift door opened to emit the Mitty's spouse.

"Admiral," Shella began forcefully, "I would strongly encourage you to engage the Skip Drive at the earliest opportunity."

"Lieutenant Heinz, plot a course for our next jump destination. Lieutenant Daniels, be ready to execute the jump on a moment's notice... but not before I give the word."

"Belay that Mister Daniels! Jump as soon as you have a jump solution," Shella ordered.

Chapter 17: Teaching Old Dogs New Tricks…

You could have heard a pin drop. Not a breath was taken by a living soul on the bridge. I turned slowly to face the Archon. There was unrepentant fury in my eyes. Shella must have seen it because she took a step back.

"No one… and I do mean no one… gives an order on this ship that countermands one of mine. Explain yourself or find yourself in the brig. Am I clear?" I said in a surprisingly calm and quiet voice.

"Admiral," Shella pleaded. "There is only one reason a race like the Tas would be engaging us. If I take the time to fully explain it to you, we may well all be dead. I'm asking you to trust me."

"Lieutenant, execute the jump as soon as Sandy has some numbers for you."

"Aye, Sir. I have the numbers… jumping now," Daniels responded.

I felt a familiar pressure at the base of my teeth and then the ship entered Skip Space.

"OK, Ambassador. Let's hear why you felt it was necessary to usurp my authority in the middle of a crisis situation. And to be clear, your continued freedom of movement on this ship is completely dependent on what I think of your answer."

"Understood, Admiral," Shella said. "Can we retire to your Ready room?"

"Negative," I said. "You challenged a commanding officer in front of his crew. You will explain yourself in front of that same crew."

Shella nodded.

"Sir, the Tas are a peaceful race, unless attacked. Therefore, the only reason they would attack a..."

"Galactic Order ship... is if they had been attacked by the Galactic Order," I finished for her when it became obvious where she was going.

"Exactly, Sir. You have to understand; the Tas are a bit of a mystery to the Galactic Order. We know they are primarily miners that trade what they mine. We also know that they have access to very advanced technology. Technology that they did not develop on their own."

"When you say advanced... was the *Gilboa* in significant danger?"

Shella looked at me with eyes wider than I had ever seen on either of the Archons.

"Admiral, those missiles that they were going to launch would have come at us at a sizeable fraction of the speed of light."

"OK, I understand that. Our HVMs do the same thing. Our point defense lasers are designed to target incoming missiles traveling at those types of speeds."

Shella looked at Mitty.

"He doesn't seem to understand," she pleaded with her husband.

The hologram stepped forward.

"Sir, if I may?"

"Go ahead. What is it I don't understand?"

"Admiral, the neutronium tips on their missiles are almost a centimeter thick."

"And this is important because?" I prompted.

"The neutronium on each of their thirty-two missiles represent about ten times the entire mass of the *Gilboa*."

I sat back and looked at the two Archons.

"Each missile has ten times the mass of the *Gilboa*? How in the hell do they fire the things? How do they keep the recoil from blowing them backwards? How does a ship that size manage to even carry one of the damns things... much less two?"

"As I say," Shella replied, "They have access to some very advanced technology."

I stood up and offered a hand to Shella. The Archon had become familiar with the human tradition of handshaking, so she reached out and shook it with a padded paw.

"I owe you an apology Ambassador. It seems you might well have saved the ship."

"Negative Admiral. I was the one who put the ship in danger by not being here to share what I knew about this species in a timely manner."

"Ambassador, my parents weren't able to teach me much, but they taught me this much... to embrace my mistakes and learn from them. It's a simple fact that the best command decisions are made with the best and most complete information is available. Sadly, that isn't always possible.

"Today was an example of what can happen when the needed information is delayed in getting to the person charged with making the command decisions - me. Had you not been willing to stand up to me and force the issue… you and I might very well be having this discussion in the hereafter.

"In this particular case, I should have anticipated that I would not know… what I did not know… if that makes any sense. Effective immediately, during ship-wide alerts your duty station is on the bridge to function as a cultural advisor.

"If, in your opinion, I am making a decision based on incomplete or faulty information… you are to 'suggest' a different course of action. The only reason we are here today is because you said… and I'm quoting you… *'I'm asking you to trust me.'*"

Shella wrinkled her nose.

"Thank you, Admiral. I promise I will not abuse your trust."

***

The next four hours were spent in the Ready room. There were a lot of unanswered questions before we left the Sol system. Now it seemed as if there were several more.

"So, tell me again," Whiskers asked. "Where do ya think the Tas got their pretty toys?"

Mitty swiveled his chair to face the Chief Engineer.

"They are not toys and as to their beauty… the Tas do not allow visitors for any reason. No one has actually been able to see the technology they use to power their ships or mine exotics like neutronium."

Whiskers waved with the back of his hand.

"Ya know what I mean. Tell me about them 'Ancestor' guys."

"In life, I knew next to nothing about them. The *Gilboa's* archaeological database makes reference to eight discoveries of ancient technology on various worlds within what you refer to as the Beehive stellar cluster. Most of these worlds are barren and orbit suns that have entered the final phases of their lifecycles.

"In almost every case, the technology was damaged, incomplete or otherwise inoperable. We believe these artifacts are remnants of an older civilization that migrated out from the core of our galaxy. It is possible that we are their offspring… and it is equality possible that they are extinct or have moved on. In any case, the technology in question is referred to as Ancestor technology," Mitty answered.

I leaned forward. I had heard something this time that I had missed before.

"Mitty, you said… 'In almost every case.' Does that mean that functional Ancestor technology has been recovered?"

"Sadly, no, Admiral. In one case, an object was found… A small one… no bigger than your hand. It still had a functional power-cell. A J'ni that was part of the recovery team attempted to activate the device. The resulting explosion destroyed the entire excavation site and any other potential artifacts that might have been found there. The crater that was formed was four-point-eight of your kilometers deep."

Note to self… don't fiddle with Ancestor tech without a reliable user's guide.

Shelby, who thankfully had taken the time to change back into her uniform, spoke up.

"It's your thought that the Tas have access to working Ancestor technology. With that sizable of an advantage… why aren't they running the show? Why aren't they in charge?"

I looked over to Shella. As I suspected, this was a question she was prepared to answer.

"The Tas are miners and traders. They have no desire or interest in ruling or being ruled. Honestly, if there was a single race in or near the Galactic Order that I would trust to have Ancestor technology… it would be the Tas."

"Maybe that's why they have it," I said.

"Beg'n the Admiral's pardon," Whiskers said, "But how do ya figure that?"

"Imagine you were the Ancestors. Your race has lived through the birth and death of stars. You are curious and inventive… as a result, your society is advanced beyond the comprehension of most other intelligent races you encounter. You move out of the galactic core and start exploring and inhabiting worlds nearer the fringe of the galaxy.

"You bring your technology with you. At some point, you've seen all the sights and you move on again… maybe to another galaxy perhaps. The point is, you don't want to take everything with you… but you know that leaving matches for the kids to play with is a good way to burn the house down. So, you hide the matches - metaphorically.

"What better race to hide Ancestor technology than peaceful race of miners. You make a covenant with them. Bury your dangerous technology where it can't be found, and we'll give you some of the best tools for mining that you can imagine."

Mike shook his head.

"I don't buy it JD," the Marine said. "Absolute power corrupts absolutely."

"That may be true for most of us… but what if the Ancestors could build a genetic imperative into their servant race. Certain species on Earth seem to exhibit genetic memory. Even human babies know how to suckle without being taught," I responded. The more I thought about it, the more I was convinced I was on the right track.

I stood up and walked around the conference table to gaze out the simulated window. The now familiar pattern of stars streaking by was captivating. Shella had told me that what I was seeing was a simulation. If I was actually about to see out the walls of the Gilboa; the discordant nature of what I would be seeing would likely drive me insane.

Creatures from our space-time frame were not designed by the Creator to handle and perceive five-dimension space.

I used the moment to think. "Question," I said. "Is it possible that whoever or whatever our adversary... our enemy is, that they have access to Ancestor tech?"

"It may also be that they are seeking additional Ancestor technology and attempted to acquire it by force from the Tas. When that didn't work they decided to explore Galactic Order space," Shelby added.

Shella and Mitty wrinkled their noses in unison. I had begun to suspect that the gesture might have a host of meanings depending on the situation. In this case, it meant they were thinking about something.

"It would seem to correlate with the available facts," Mitty speculated. "It is possible that they discovered and managed to utilize a small artifact that caused them to thoroughly explore whatever region of space they occupy. Having exhausted that avenue of investigation they broaden their investigation."

"I suspect," Shella added, "that the Commander might have the order of advance backwards."

"It's certainly possible," Shelby admitted. "You're thinking that because the Tas attacked us that somehow the Galactic Order has been coopted into joining the search?"

The Archon nodded. "The Tas are a peaceful - if reclusive race. I think it is unlikely that they would suddenly attack any and all ships showing up near one of their dig sites... Especially as we have enjoyed peaceful relations for hundreds of years."

"And they would still want and need trading partners," Whiskers offered.

"Good point," I said. "It does bring up another issue. Mitty mentioned that the Tas were not known to be in the star system we just visited. Either is was just random chance that they were there or there is something there that they wanted to protect."

"Which means," Shella added, "that if you are correct, Admiral, their attack on the *Gilboa* may not have been motivated by animosity towards the Galactic Order but rather a desire to guard their charge against all comers… much like a mother Mutic guards her chicks."

"OK," I said. "We have a working hypothesis based on some rather sketchy facts and more speculation than I am comfortable with. Let's do what we can to gather more information to fill in the gaps and either prove our hypothesis or replace it with a better one."

We spoke for a few more minutes but eventually the meeting broke up.

***

A week later we approached our next Skip Space exit. In a way I was glad we had run into the Tas. The experience taught this old dog new tricks. It turned out we would need them sooner than I had hoped.

Chapter 18: Dog Cage...

"Red Alert!" I yelled. The *Gilboa* rocked as a series of recently cloaked weapons platforms lit up her enhanced shields.

We had exited Skip Space on schedule. The system we were entering consisted of a trio of G-type stars orbiting a distant black hole. It was this massive black hole that required our dropping out of Skip Space. A gravity well of this magnitude disrupted the space-time waves used to travel in Skip Space much like a reef disrupted ocean waves.

Our intent was to use the nearest of the orbiting suns to provide a gravity assist to propel us far enough from the black hole to safely reengage our FTL drive. What we hadn't anticipated was that a system with a black hole was the perfect place for would-be attackers to lay in wait.

Shortly before we engaged our VASIMR drives to begin our sling-shot maneuver, the weapons platforms decloaked and began firing on us. Had the *Gilboa* not had significantly enhanced shields there is no question in my mind that the power and intensity of the attack would have doomed the ship. It was clear that the Beehive had become a very dangerous place.

"Weapons, lock onto the nearest platform and give it a full spread of our plasma beams. Take them out. I need them to know that we mean business."

"Aye Admiral," the young ensign replied crisply.

I would have felt better if Colonel Morrison was at the firing button, but he was running his Marines through yet another series of boarding simulations.

Twelve Plasma beams lashed out. Each one operated at one-hundred and thirty Petajoules. They hit the targeted platform. Its own shields lasted for a fraction of a second before they turned from amber to bright white and then failed. The weapons platform itself lasted only a fraction of a second longer before it essentially disintegrated.

The remaining platforms ceased fire.

"Sir," Mitty said. "We are being hailed. The sentient calling is a Rohar. Its title is Supreme Guardian. They are an androgynous race that are highly territorial. Their function within the Galactic Order is that of picketing and planetary guards."

"We are being attacked by members of the Galactic Order?" I asked. "That doesn't make any sense."

"It does if the Galactic Order has fallen and is now fragmented," Mitty relied. "Shall I answer their hail?"

I turned to Shella. "Ambassador, anything I should know?"

She wrinkled her nose before answering. "As my husband indicated, they are a highly territorial race. They are also considered somewhat harsh and lacking in anything even remotely like a sense of humor. They take offense at the littlest affront. I'm baffled as to why they would attack a ship of the Order… unless, as it has been suggested, the local political environment has shifted. I would talk with them but be prepared for more hostilities."

"Mitty, open a channel – audio only."

Immediately a harsh voice pounded out of the speakers on the bridge.

"…interlopers must leave. Our battle fleet approaches. We will destroy you."

I straightened in my command chair.

"Attention Supreme Guardian. I am Fleet Admiral Jeremy Riker of the Galactic Order's Battleship *Gilboa*. Your attack was unwarranted. We mean you no harm and only wish to use this system to transit to our next jump point. We will, however, defend ourselves. Please acknowledge."

"What nonsense it this? There is no more Galactic Order."

"That's news to us. Care to enlighten us as to what has happened?"

Rather than answering my question, the Rohar on the other ship made a barking noise that was very guttural. The *Gilboa* did not translate it so I wasn't sure it was even intended to be speech.

"Turn on your video feed that I might look upon the face of the creature lying to me," the Supreme Guardian said at last.

I nodded to Mitty. A flat holographic display shimmered into existence about six feet in front of my command chair.

The creature in front of me appeared to be some type of lizard. Its skin was almost black and its eyes (it had the standard issue two) seemed to be compound multifaceted organs with thousands of individual lenses… not unlike the eyes on a housefly. My near-perfect memory recalled that compound eyes were able to detect both the polarization of light and colors. For flies at least, this meant they could recognize even the slightest movements in a wide field of view. I could see how this would be useful in an aggressive species.

I addressed the Supreme Guardian again.

"I hope this sates your curiosity. This ship has been gone for a very long time. What happened that causes you to say the Galactic Order has fallen?"

The image of the Guardian stepped closer to the screen. I could see thick drool dripping from its mouth... not unlike a Komodo Dragon on Earth.

"What species are you?"

I was getting tired of having my questions ignored.

"I'd be happy to tell you all about ourselves but first I want some answers from you. What happened. Why are you claiming the Galactic Order is no more?"

A long, bifurcated, tongue extended from the creature's mouth and wiped away some of the drool. It seemed to be an automatic gesture like blinking one's eyes to keep the cornea moist.

"The Order fell in battle to a more powerful opponent," the Rohar said is a raspy voice. "There was no dishonor, they fought bravely, if ineptly. Are you returning in order to surrender yourselves and your ship to the victors?"

"Not a chance it hell," I replied. "By the way. I honor my promises. I and most of my crew are of a race known as humans."

The Supreme Guardian made the same barking noise it had made earlier. I was of the opinion it made this type of noise in response to something unexpected. After the barking ran its course, the Rohar addressed me again.

"Human Fleet Admiral Jeremy Riker, your news is unexpected. I would talk with you directly."

"I'm not sure I follow?" I wondered if he was asking to come over to the *Gilboa*?

The Guardian licked more drool before responding.

"I would invite you and a small party to join me on my ship. I see one of the Archons with you. It appears to be unencumbered. I suspect you will need protective suits as our worlds have richer atmospheres than you will likely be comfortable with. Is this agreeable?"

I leaned forward and rubbed my chin. "Supreme Guardian. I thank you for your offer. I need a few minutes to consult with my crew."

Again, I heard the barking noise. It seemed more violent this time... almost as if there was a hint of anger or irritation in it.

"We are not known as a patient people, Human Fleet Admiral Jeremy Riker. Respond soon or lose the offer."

I signaled Mitty to mute the signal.

Shella walked up to my chair.

"Admiral, I would advise against traveling to their ship. You saw how testy the Rohar was. If you were there in person, you could easily come to harm without even knowing your offense."

"I agree but there is another issue at hand. We need answers… and right now the only answers to be had are," I gestured with my hand towards the viewscreen, "over there."

"Then might I recommend taking me with you to help to avoid unfortunate cultural missteps."

I shook my head. "I'm afraid not Ambassador. It's not that you wouldn't be immensely valuable but the risk to your person would be too great. The away team will consist of myself, Colonel Morrison and Mitty."

***

It turns out that 'richer atmosphere' meant that the Rohar's *preferred* atmospheric mix included low levels of ammonia… something on the order of one-hundred and fifty parts per million. That level of exposure would tend to cause serious lung damage to an unprotected human if they were exposed to it for even ten or fifteen minutes.

Our protective suits would be a new type of Marine Encounter Suit developed on Earth using Galactic Order technology and fabricators. They weren't known for their comfort, but they were strong, and could take a beating. In addition, they had self-contained environmental systems including rebreathers.

In the old days we would have used spacesuits. Our Mark-One MES offered much better protection. In addition, the Rohar would not have seen them in action and therefore would have no idea as to their capabilities. If they decided to take offense at something we did or said, the suits might give us a chance to extricate ourselves from the situation.

I was hoping that it wouldn't come to fighting our way out. We needed information and allies more than we needed another fight. Sadly, hope and reality sometimes intersect at a thing called disappointment... at least temporarily.

The *Gilboa* had sixteen shuttles of Galactic Order design as well as four much larger and more heavily shielded human-designed assault craft or ACs.

The ACs had been battle-tested in that last dust-up over Mars. The only real difference was the retro-fitting of a Galactic Order fusion core and shield emitters. Luxuries like gravity plating and more powerful plasma turrets would have to wait for the next round of upgrades... or more likely, the design of an entirely new assault craft.

I bring all of this up because in hindsight – often my best view – I really wish we had flown one of the ACs. The shuttles we used were faster and had the advantage of being something familiar to the Rohar... but we might as well have flown over in a paper bag for all the protection they provided.

The trip to the Rohar weapons platform took about thirty minutes. Just about the perfect amount of time required to feel and appreciate that twist in your gut –as you watch the alien station bristling with hot weapons systems slowly track your every move.

Did I mention *how much* the Galactic Order shuttle filled me with confidence in its defensive capabilities?

As a child I had visited my grandfather's hunting cabin up near Owen Sound, Ontario. The cabin had an outhouse for doing your business. My grandfather swore it was part of the 'roughing it' experience. One day I was engaged in 'said business' when I heard a bear outside rummaging around the little shed; doing whatever it is bears do around outhouses when little boys are trying take a dump. My gut felt the same way then that it did now.

At last the shuttle docked on the Rohar platform. The platform was a fraction of the size of the *Gilboa*. That said, there were dozens of them in this section of the star system. Heaven alone knew how many existed in other parts of the system.

In a certain way, their presence here made sense. The gravity well produced by the black hole was kind of a 'honey pot' that would draw in ships from Skip Space. This would, in effect, allow the Rohar to act like the bouncers at a bar; to keep undesirables out of Galactic Order space. The million-dollar question was – with the Galactic Order possibly defunct, what were the Rohar doing by aggressively defending the honey pot?

It took the Guardians less than thirty seconds to surround the shuttle once it had touched down and the hanger bay clamps latched onto the landing supports. I watched them swarm the area around the shuttle on a viewscreen that showed the exterior of our craft. There had to be twenty of them out there.

I looked over at Mike. He gave me a thumbs-up and the two other Marines that he had insisted come with us, stood and flanked the door.

The Rohar were imposing to say the least. At almost two hundred pounds, they stood about seven feet tall when standing on their rear legs. Apparently, God issued them four in total plus a single set of two arms. When they stood on all four-leg s, which they were doing now, they were still five feet tall. Their hands had four opposable digits.

According to Mitty, they were cold-blooded but typically wore heated clothing that kept their bodies at a toasty one hundred and one degrees Fahrenheit. My thought in bringing Mitty was to use him as an advisor for dealing with the Rohar. Sadly, the best laid plans of mice and men sometimes are for naught. This was one of those times.

I had Mitty's holographic emitter tucked away in my armor. It was a transceiver unit like the one I had used when we first met Admiral Spratt on Lunar Two. That meant Mitty, himself, was still safely aboard the *Gilboa*. I needed his advice, so I tried to access Mitty on my comms. That was when I discovered that our connection to the *Gilboa* had been severed. I guess Mitty wouldn't be joining us on this trip after all.

The ones that came to 'escort' us were wearing some type of ceramic armor that looked like scales. If it weren't for the abundance of obvious bits of technology stuck willy-nilly here and there on their suits, I might have mistaken the armor for some type of flexible shell like an armadillo had. The only part of the Rohars that were exposed were their long snouts. I presume this was so that they could drool freely without getting the inside of their armor wet.

Each carried what could only be some type of rifle. I didn't know if they threw slugs or some type of energy beam. Frankly, and I say this with all sincerity, I hoped never to find out.

Our hosts escorted us down a long dark corridor. We tried greeting them, but our escort was not interested in talking… except of course for the barking noise they made when startled or agitated or ticked-off that dinner was late.

Apparently the Rohar also didn't like a lot of light. Either that or they were adapted to use a significantly different spectrum of light. I adjusted the optical sensors in my MES's helmet display. This allowed me to see a broader range of light frequencies. To my astonishment, there was not a lot of light period. I would learn later that the dragons, as I had begun to think of them, used smell almost as much as they used their eyes to navigate.

Since I wasn't going to be able to use my tongue to find my way around (and as a point of clarification… I wouldn't have even if I could!); I opted to augment the available light with a dim ultra-violet emitter mounted on my chest plate. The Rohar didn't react when I turned it on, so I was hopeful they weren't seeing it.

My ongoing worry was that we would offend them in some manner. For all I knew, they might feel that the use of additional light was offensive. To make matters worse… I had no idea if the dragons would honor a parley truce.

After about ten minutes of walking, we finally came to a room where it seemed we would meet some of the Rohar that were actually interested in having a conversation. The dragons in this room were quite a bit stockier than the ones that had escorted us. Also, these Rohar wore what I can only assume were uniforms.

The room held three of the Guardians. I recognized the Supreme Guardian from the holographic display on the *Gilboa*.

I decided to take the initiative and speak first. What can I say? I'm given to reckless flights of fantasy upon occasion. I had a grand 'delusion' that we and the Rohar were going to be able to work together amicably.

"Greetings, Supreme Guardian. I am Admiral Riker."

The immediate response was more of the aforementioned guttural barking; followed by something I was hoping not to hear…

"Silence! The accused will be silent."

Chapter 19: Lost Dog…

"I think there might be a misunderstanding here," I said in the hopes of defusing the situation.

One of the armored guards took that opportunity to whack me on the back of the head with something that seemed pretty solid. Thank the Lord for our own armor. If I hadn't been wearing it, I'm not sure I would have survived the blow. These guys were playing for keeps.

Sadly, or fortunately, depending on how you looked at it; one of Mike's Marines decided to go red-shirt. Before Mike or I could stop him, he turned and planted a servo-enhanced fist in the snout of the dragon that had struck me. The result was spectacular.

Apparently, dragons had glass-jaws. The Rohar in question crumbled like a house of cards being toppled over. This, of course, precipitated a knock-down, drag-out fight between the Rohar escort and the crew of the *Gilboa*.

It wasn't much of a fight. There was a hell of a lot more of them then there were of us. Still, we acquitted ourselves rather nicely. I don't mean to brag – well actually I do – but I took down almost as many of the dragons as Colonel Morrison; and we were heads and dragon tails above the other Marines. Still, five-to-one odds were hard to overcome.

Thankfully, everybody was playing nice – a relative term I know – and not using weapons besides mark-one fists and, in the case of the dragons, the butt end of their rifles.

The melee was over when one of our opponents got a lucky hit on Mike and knocked his helmet off. The way his eyes bulged when he took that first breath of what the Rohar's called air told me I wasn't going to enjoy experiencing it on my own.

As my friend stepped back to reattach his helmet, three of the dragons pinned my arms. The rest of Mike's men as well as Mike himself, soon found themselves similarly restrained.

The three Rohar officers had stayed out of the fight. Whether this was because they were not wearing armor or because such fighting was beneath them... I couldn't say. At any rate, once we were restrained, the leader began to talk.

To be honest, I wish this had been where we had started things. Sadly, no one ever consults me on things like this.

"I am pleased to see you humans are a people with a strong scent. It is a refreshing change. I promise you that your end will be one with honor," the Supreme Guardian said.

I had no idea at the time what the reference to 'strong scent' was all about, but that thing about 'ending with honor' was all too clear... and I wasn't a fan.

"See, there you go again being negative," I spat. "Why can't we just have a conversation like civilized people. We have no idea what is going on and aside from unprovoked threats, you've not been very forthcoming. I'm beginning to think you are trying to piss me off."

I had expected any number of reactions, but a very human type of laugh was not among them. Oh, don't get me wrong, the laugh was much deeper than a human could have produced, and it was accompanied by quite a bit more spittle... but a laugh it most certainly was.

"Admiral Riker, I sense we could have been good friends. I must talk with my officers and decide what is a fitting fate. You are not personally responsible for the evils done to my people, but you now represent an organization that we are at war with."

He sent some unseen signal to his men. Before I could say anything else, we were half-dragged, half-carried out of the room. Five minutes later, we found ourselves in a brig that could have found a home on any ship in the Federated Fleet. I guess certain engineering problems lend themselves to a universal set of solutions. As the solid door closed with an ominous clunk, we could hear the dragons marching off. We couldn't know for sure, but it seemed like they hadn't bothered to leave any guards posted by the door.

Thankfully, the dragons had let us keep our MES gear. Apparently, they didn't want us to die of asphyxiation until they could agree how to kill us. I appreciated that. It was the little acts of kindness that made such a difference in the world.

Mike and I looked at each other. I was pretty sure that we were being monitored, but I doubted the Rohar knew how to interpret sign-language. I signaled that we needed to locate and disable the monitoring devices.

The four of us began a systematic search of the cell we had been placed in. It turned out that each of the corners had very small cameras located where the ceiling and two walls came together. Our MES gear included a supply of duct tape, affectionately known as 100 mph tape. A small piece in each corner solved the camera issue.

There was still the possibility that additional cameras where hidden about the room, so Mike had one of his boys... I think it was Corporal Ramirez, apply a mark-one fist to each of the lighting fixtures.

Now that the room was dark, we turned on our headlamps... tuning them to the frequency of light that I had used earlier. It seemed probable that the Rohar weren't able to see in such conditions.

Now that we had done our best to secure our privacy, we began to plan our escape. We continued to use sign language because we couldn't know how well our hosts were able to monitor our comms as well as acoustics.

"We need to find a way out of here," Mike signed.

I nodded. One thing was sure... the *Gilboa* was not going to be much help. Any action they took would very likely result in our deaths. As I looked around I saw few if any opportunities for escaping. This, of course, made sense as 'containment' was the primary function of a jail cell.

"Ideas?"

"It's a good bet force is not going to do the job," the Colonel responded.

"Yeah, that's what I was thinking. The door has a mechanical latch, so we won't be shorting it out. How about the ceiling?" I asked.

"It's worth checking into. Whatever we do, we need to do it quickly. I can't imagine our slobbering friends are going to leave us alone for that long now that we have disabled their cameras."

I waved Corporal Ramirez over. Mike explained what we were after and then the two of us boosted him up towards the ceiling. This was the same trick we had used to smash the lights to begin with.

The Corporal felt along the edge of the light fixture. Eventually he found a recessed clasp which released the panel. Fortunately, Private Ryan caught the falling fixture before it could hit the ground.

What was left in the ceiling was a two-foot by four-foot rectangular hole. There was no way of knowing if it led anywhere but as our options were limited; we could stay where we were and die... or go spelunking through an alien spacecraft... I opted for the high-adventure route.

We formed a ladder. The Private climbed up us and entered the hole in the ceiling first. He then pulled up the Corporal.

At this point, it was just the Colonel and I left in the room. Mike signaled for me to step into his hand and he would toss me up, so the others could catch me and pull me the rest of the way. I nixed the idea. I ordered Mike to step into my clasped hands. He shook his head. I thought I was going to have a mutiny rather than a foot on my hands.

I explained that the three Marines would make a better rescue team for me—should the need arise, than I would with two enlisted that I barely knew.

Mike reluctantly conceded the logic. He stepped into my hand and I gave him a servo assisted toss to the air. Private Ryan and Corporal Ramirez caught each of his arms and pulled him the rest of the way up.

Next, I grabbed the light panel and tossed it up to the others. The idea was we would replace it on our way out. With luck this would delay our hosts as they tried to discover how we escaped. That had been our plan at any rate. It was a good plan as far as it went... sadly, it did not go far enough.

Mike and Ramirez were holding onto Private Ryan's legs and just beginning to lower him back down into the brig, so I could jump up and use him as a Marine rope... when I heard the sound of approaching dragon feet. Their four-footed gate made a very unique sound.

I hand-signed for Mike to pull the Private up and reset the light panel. I proceeded to sit on one of the three rectangular blocks situated about the cell. I tried to look bored... at least as bored as a man can look while wearing a Marine Encounter Suit.

The panel was just falling into place when I heard the door mechanism begin to open. I debated trying to rush the guards that entered but I decided there was a time to be foolish and a time to be smart... this was most likely a time for the second and not the first.

The dragon that opened the door was none other than my good buddy the Supreme Guard himself.

*　*　*

I have to say, my second meeting with the old boy went a hell of a lot better than the first. It turned out the Rohar detested weakness. They hated interacting with races they deemed as having no scent. It seemed the stronger the Rohar, the more drool they produced... the more scent they scattered. Seriously, the sign of a powerful Rohar is the amount of slobber they can generate – ya can't make stuff like this up.

They tolerated membership in the Galactic Order only because membership brought advantages to their people and at the same time there was no requirement to interact with the weaker races. The whole 'take offense at the drop of a hat' façade was a way for them to retain a sense of isolation.

By fighting back and then subsequently escaping confinement, we had established ourselves as a race worthy in their eyes.

It had taken me about six hours to contact the Colonel again. The Marines had gone radio silent as per protocol. Every six hours they would turn their radios on for sixty seconds. I had my MES send a recall message every fifteen seconds.

In the six hours we were out of contact, Mike and his men had left a surprisingly long line of tasered and bound dragons in their wake. It seemed they were trying to make their way back to the shuttle… presumably to call for reinforcements.

Every time a new bunch of bound Rohar were discovered and reported, NicNic, which was the Supreme Guard's name, would burst out into laughter. After this happened for the seventh or eighth time, I resolved to have the engineering team install visor wiper blades… just to handle the spittle that kept covering me.

Mike had the last laugh it seemed. As the six-hour blackout window opened up, I was finally able to converse with my Marine Commander. It appeared the trail of tasered dragons had been a ruse.

"Colonel Morrison, you can stand down," I said over the comms as I finally got a channel open indicator.

"Queen to Queen's level Three," came the cryptic response.

I looked over at NicNic. The Rohar was either the best alien actor that I had ever met, or we could trust them. The bottom line was we needed information and allies more than we needed safety. With that in mind, I gave the correct counter sign.

"Queen to King's Level One. I believe we may have found some allies."

"Understood sir. I've been monitoring your situation closely for the last several hours. If you'd inform our host that I'll be arriving shortly; I'd take it as a kindness if his soldiers would abstain from shooting me."

I looked at NicNic again as I checked my friend's location on my HUD. Now that his locator beacon was back on, I could see that he was indeed close... very close.

"The Colonel is about to stop by. He'd appreciate it if your men didn't shoot him when he arrived," I said with a grin.

NicNic barked an order at one of the two guards in the room. The Roharian soldier started to move towards the door to relay the command to the guards outside.

I held up my hand. "I beg your forgiveness Supreme Guardian. When I said, 'stop by' I should have said 'drop in'."

I'm not sure what was louder. The ruckus made by the falling light panel or the Supreme Guardian's laughter.

Chapter 20: Making Friends with the Dog...

Back on the *Gilboa* I held a senior staff meeting. A representative of the Rohar was also in attendance. It seemed the dragons had an easier time breathing our air than we did theirs. The Roharian emissary was sensitive to the intensity of light we used on the *Gilboa*, so he wore specially fitted contact lens that both filtered the light coming into his eyes. In addition, the lenses provided an augmented reality overlay that allowed him to read the English script that now dominated the *Gilboa's* electronic displays.

 The emissary's name was unpronounceable. Whiskers suggested we call him Jowls and surprisingly the emissary liked the name.

Jowls stood at the conference table rather than sitting. It seemed with four legs to stand on, sitting was too much of a bother. As a concession to the sensibilities of other races, the emissary stopped the excessive drooling that characterized their race.

Apparently, the drooling was under voluntary control... much like a human spitting. Remembering the amount of slime, the Supreme Guardian had covered me with, during the course of our second conversation, I vowed to address the issue man-to-dragon the next time I saw him.

The emissary began laying out what happened while the *Gilboa* was searching for help.

I knew most of what was going to be shared but I needed the rest of my senior staff to know what we were facing. Having Jowls conduct the briefing would accomplish two things. First, it would afford me a second perspective on the events of the last year or so in Galactic Order space – I already had the Supreme Guardian's take on the events that had transpired. Second, it would give my crew a chance to learn what the Rohar were really like.

The Archons, Mitty and Shella, had been shocked to learn that the dragons had a sense of humor and were actually very easy to get along with once you had earned their respect.

"Once the Saulites were effectively eliminated by a specially crafted virus, the Galactic Order fell into disarray. An armada of strange ships began sweeping the quadrant. Some worlds they would completely ignore. Others they would attack. It seemed completely random.

"Our home world was one of the last ravaged. The enemy used our own Galactic Order ships against us. To this day, we do not know if the people crewing those ships were from the Galactic Order or if they were this mysterious enemy.

"We attempted to defend ourselves. After the Saulite, the Rohar were the only military force left in the Galactic Order. The problem was our operations had always been defensive and never intended to ward off an invasion fleet, especially not one augmented by the resources of our own allies.

"To make matters worse, the enemy seemed to have access to better technology. We could beat them but only when several ships concentrated their fire on a single enemy craft. We captured a few Saulite attack vessels and attempted to mount a more credible defense, but, in the end, we were too few.

"After a devastating space battle that saw most of our soldiers killed, our homeworld fell. The enemy paid dearly for their victory, but then, so did we. Much of our world is a nuclear wasteland. From what we have been able to determine, the same is true for other worlds that attempted to resist the incursion.

"Those of us who survived made it our business to... how do you humans say it? Make the bastards pay. We already controlled several of the natural Skip Space sinks... ones like the system we are in now.

"If a large armada comes through we remain hidden. If a single ship or even a small group passes through, we take them out. Yours is the first ship to come through that we were not able to easily destroy with our fixed-weapons platform. I'd be curious to know how you defended yourselves so ably."

I leaned forward. "Humans are somewhat unusual in that we can excel at a number of tasks. Once we had access to Galactic Order technology, we were able to see ways to improve upon it. The *Gilboa* is the result of those enhancements."

"I see," Jowls said. "Our partnership may well be a God-sent. With the help of humanity, we may be able to turn the tide of this war... even at this late hour."

"That is certainly my intent," I added.

"Tell me, Jowls, do your people have any idea who this enemy is or even what they want?" Colonel Morrison asked.

I smiled slightly. Those had been the very questions I was going to ask next.

The emissary actuated the conference table's holographic display.

"These are representations of the types of ships that attacked our world. The *Gilboa* is displayed to provide a sense of scale. As you can see, with the exception of the Birther ship, all are considerably smaller than the *Gilboa*. That said, they each pack as much firepower as several of our more powerful ships. We have never seen the Birther fire its weapons but given the number of gun ports visible on its hull, we estimate its firepower exceeds that of the combined swarm of attack craft that launch from its hangers.

"We have never been able to communicate with them. Their mode of operation is almost always the same. They arrive and attack. They never ask for terms. They conquer a planet and then begin mining operations."

Shella spoke for the first time in our meeting.

"You said 'Their mode of operation is almost always the same'. By always, I'm assuming the sterilization of the Saulites and Archon homeworld, represent the deviations from their standard operating procedures."

"That is correct Ambassador. As for why the deviation… we are not adept at tactics."

"Do we know what they were mining for?" I asked although I had a suspicion I knew what the answer was going to be.

Jowls used his tongue to taste the air. I think that was the dragon's way of rubbing their chins in thought.

"It's very odd. We see them dig a lot of dirt and rock. Sometimes a cargo hauler, one of ours, will make landfall and then shortly depart. There never appears to be enough time between touchdown and takeoff to load much onto the hauler. Many times, once the hauler departs, the enemy also abandons the dig."

I nodded. Jowls had added a new piece to the puzzle.

"You said many times. What are the exceptions?"

"There is only one that I am aware of. In the case of the Archon homeworld, a massive dig was conducted... one that dwarfed what we have seen on other worlds. No hauler ever landed but once the digging was done... the enemy glassed the entire dig site with high-yield fusion bombs."

Again, I nodded.

"This would tend to confirm our working theory," I said to the group.

Now it was Jowl's turn to ask us a question. I proceeded to explain our speculation as to what the unknown enemy was doing. That they had somehow come into possession of a limited amount of Ancestor technology and were hellbent on acquiring more.

I told the emissary about our encounter with the normally peaceful Tas and our speculation that they may in fact be agents of the Ancestors tasked with hiding Ancestor artifacts.

It was Mike that brought up the elephant in the room. If we were fighting an adversary that had access to Ancestor tech then the best way to counter them would be to have access to our own cache on Ancestor tech.

"If such delights were available for the taking... they'd already be taken... if ya get my drift," Whiskers said.

I smiled. Whiskers caught the twinkle in my eye and asked me point-blank; *what was the insane plan I had just come up with.* I told them.

***

"Admiral on the bridge," Commander Shelby barked crisply as I exited the turbolift.

"As you were," I said with mild annoyance.

I had almost broken my First Officer of this particular habit but the arrival of the Roharian emissary had rekindled her adherence to protocol. I responded by grabbing a bag of popcorn and munching it loudly was I sat in my command chair. When she walked over to my chair I offered the bag to her. As expected, she declined.

"Orders, Admiral?"

"Are the Roharian ships ready?" I asked. My plan, such as it was depended on the Rohar.

"Affirmative. They were able to scrape together eight ships. There are four more that our engineering staff says could be made battle-ready with a few more weeks of time and effort."

"The eight will have to do. We don't even know if the Tas are going to be willing to talk with us… much less agree to retrofit our ships with their missile tech."

"Understood. I'll let the engineering staff know to close down repair operations on the remaining Roharian ships. We should be able to get underway within the hour," Shelby said.

"Very good Number One. Please advise both of our Ambassadors that their duty stations will be on the bridge during any alien contact situations."

"I anticipated your order, Sir. I have had engineering reconfigure two of the rear bridge stations to accommodate each of the Ambassadors. Each station is configured with control surfaces and readouts that are suitable for either Archon or Roharian users. I've also taken the liberty of asking Commander McGraw to design a suitable space for a Taserite environmental module. As you might recall, they require a considerably higher atmospheric pressure than we can tolerate."

"That's exceptional work, Commander. Did Whiskers think he and his team can do it?"

"Absolutely, Sir," Commander Shelby said with the slightest of smiles. "There is only one minor change to the current bridge configuration that needs to be made."

"Great," I said. "Just for grins and kicks, what would that change be?"

"Oh, nothing critical, Sir," she answered evasively.

"Commander?"

"They'll need to remove the popcorn machine."

***

An hour and fifteen minutes later we were on our way. Nine ships led by the *Gilboa*. For the second time in my illustrious career, I was the commander of record of a fleet… only this time the ships weren't mothballed.

Chapter 21: Tricky Dog

It took us about a week to make it back to the system where we had previously encountered the Tas. As my small fleet dropped out of Skip Space, I put the first part of my plan into motion.

"Sensors, do a full active scan. Light us up like a Christmas tree. If the Tas are still here I want them to see us."

"Aye, Admiral," Ensign MacDonald replied crisply. "Full scan initiated. Initial data should be returning from the nearest planetary body in roughly six minutes. Passive scans show no foreign ships within range of our optical systems."

"Very good, Ensign. Engineering, you know what to do the moment we get a sensor ping back from that Taserite task force?"

"Absolutely, Admiral. And I hope this works. If it doesn't it's going to be worse than piss'n into the wind."

"Thank you for that lovely image, Engineer. If this goes south, I'll die with that comforting thought on my mind."

"We aim to please, Admiral," Whiskers replied smugly.

Mitty shimmered into existence next to me.

"Sir, I've run those calculations you asked me to. As expected, they took quite a while. Based on our limited knowledge of the Tas, I estimate only a sixty-eight percent chance that the *Gilboa* will not be destroyed."

"That's not so bad. Our chances of stopping the enemy from pillaging every nearby system for Ancestor artifacts without some way of leveling the playing field is near zero. I'll take a sixty-eight percent chance of success any day."

"You misunderstand my response, Admiral. I was referring only to the destruction of the *Gilboa*. Our chances of complete success are only twenty-three percent. If we allow for partial compliance with our requests the odds improve to fifty-fifty."

"There ya go, Mitty," I said with a grin and a twinkle in my eye. "Fifty-fifty are great odds in a game where the house almost always wins. Sometimes you have to commit to the dice and allow lady luck a chance to help you."

"I'm sure I don't understand what any of that means," the Archon said. "But, I trust you know what you are doing."

"Contact, Admiral," Ensign MacDonald reported. "There are a few more of them this time. Counting… Twenty-Four Taserites inbound. Same ship configuration as before."

"Thank you, Chris," I replied.

"Comms, alert the Rohar that operation 'Two Dog' is a go. Whiskers if you would be so kind as to cut power to all non-critical systems besides the running lights, I would be appreciative."

"Aye, Admiral. Going belly up, now."

***

Three minutes later the lead Tas Talon saw two Galactic Order battleships power down all their systems. One ship sat alone in space. The other was surrounded by Roharian Light Cruisers. It was a curious configuration.

They, of course, had no way of knowing the ship surrounded by the Rohar was actually a massive holographic projection. One of the reasons the *Gilboa* had powered down her non-essential systems was to reduce her electromagnetic signature so that the real ship and the decoy appeared more closely identical.

The commander of the lead Tas Talon thought hard about what he was seeing. *The Rohar were not known to be in league with the Defilers. Perhaps that had changed*.

The collective spent the several hours that it took to reach the interlopers contemplating the nature of this threat. There were several possibilities. Destruction of the invaders was deemed the best possible course of action to insure the fulfillment of the prime directive.

***

Several hours later the Tas armada was almost within weapons range. I have to admit, sitting with systems powered down was a bit of a gamble. I was betting that the Tas would take a look at our posture and at least grant us a moment to talk. In my mind, conversation was the only way we were going to win this. I tried to live by the old maxim; the best battles are the ones never fought.

"Mitty, open up a channel to those ships. Let's see if they'll talk."

"Attempting to open a channel, Admiral," the hologram replied.

And now we wait, I thought to myself.

A few moments later Mitty announced, "They are not responding, Admiral."

"Unfortunate but expected," I said. "Signal the lead Roharian ship to attempt communications."

"The Roharians are reporting a communication link has been established. The Tas are asking if the Rohar have joined with the 'Defilers'."

"Patch me into their conversation," I ordered.

As Mitty complied I heard the end of an exchange between the Tas and the Rohar. The dragon was attempting to explain that neither his command vessel nor the other ships from the Galactic Order were, in fact, in league with the unknown enemy which the Tas were calling the Defilers.

"Mitty, is it audio only or can we get a visual?"

"The Tas are only broadcasting audio."

I nodded as much to myself as to anybody else. It seemed the Tas were intent to remain enigmas. I decided to join the conversation.

"Attention, Tas commander," I said as I interrupted their conversation. "My name is Admiral Riker. I am a human from a planet called Earth that has only recently aligned with the Galactic Order. If we are going to stop these Defilers, we need information."

An electronically generated voice emanated from the bridge speakers.

"We are not familiar with a race called 'Human'. Our analysis indicates a high probability that the Defilers are also an unknown race."

"I see where you are going with this. I assure you that we are not your enemy. What can we do to convince you that we are not a threat?"

The electronic voice replied almost immediately and with no emotion. I had no way of knowing if the lack of feeling in the voice was a result of the translation or a reflection of the fundamental differences between the Tas and humans. In either case, I found their response less than comforting.

"You can allow us to destroy you."

"ADMIRAL! They're firing missiles," MacDonald reported.

"Target?"

"One moment, Sir… Target confirmed. They are targeting the ghost ship."

Barely a minute later, a pair of neutronium-tipped missiles struck and passed through the holographic clone of the *Gilboa*. The computer geeks had rigged the hologram to flare a fake set of shields to make it appear like the ship had weathered the attack unscathed.

The Tas tried three more times to kill our ghost ship. When two missiles didn't do the trick, they fired four of their little neutronium gems at it. When that didn't work, they tried twelve. Each time our fake shield flared and when it cleared, the *Gilboa's* doppelganger would still be there.

I began to worry that they would take a potshot at the other battleship, so I decided it was time to talk again.

"Tas commander, you can fire at us all day or you can allow us to have a conversation. Know this, we will not fire back as we have no desire to hurt potential allies in our fight against our common enemy, the Defilers."

No more missiles were launched. It seemed the Tas were evaluating their options for moving forward. The fact that they had stopped firing was a good thing, but it filled me with a certain amount of dread. It meant that we were going to put the next part of my plan into motion. This was the part of the plan that even I didn't like.

***

I launched my one-man personal shuttle from one of the smaller hanger bays on the *Gilboa*. This particular ship was of human design. It used old-style VASIMR thrusters that were far less powerful than the ones we had powered by Galactic Order power systems.

This was deliberate on my part. I wanted to let the Tas know that I was completely at their mercy. Of course, the downside to this plan was... I was completely at their mercy.

The Rohar, who seemed to be on better speaking terms with the Tas, informed them that I was meeting them half way. That my shuttle was unarmed and unshielded. They would be able to destroy it and its sole passenger easily. This was being done as a sign of good faith.

For untold centuries humans had been saluting other humans. Many believed the custom evolved from the time of the Romans. A raised right hand meant you were not carrying a weapon and were, therefor, safe to approach. I didn't know if the Tas had a similar concept of presenting oneself as a non-threat in order to parley. I was hoping that they did… or at least were open to learning one.

Somehow, I knew that the Tas were going to be more willing to talk with me one on one than they were across tens of thousands of miles of open space. Logically it shouldn't have made a difference, but I had learned over the years to trust my gut.

To my delight, a small transport exited one of the Tas Talons and headed in my direction. Given the vastness of space and the distances involved, I didn't see any of this but Commander Shelby on the Gilboa had Mitty send me updates from their much more capable passive sensors.

The small Tas ship was still several times the size of my vessel. It was possible that they didn't have smaller crafts, or it could simply be a matter of wanting to have a conversation from a position of strength. It didn't really matter to me. We were talking. That was the important thing.

After about twenty minutes our two ships neared each other and began breaking maneuvers. Because the Tas ship had a far more powerful set of thrusters, we were actually much closer to the *Gilboa* then we were to the Tas armada.

I had instructed the Rohar to discontinue the holographic ruse if it became clear that the Tas were going to agree to a face-to-face. I noticed our second battleship had disappeared as the small Taserite vessel made its way to me.

My viewscreen flickered and a dark grey worm appeared on the screen. I saw something that looked like it was what the Tas used for a mouth. It was a circular orifice with hundreds of thin, undulating cilia. I flicked a switch and sent a video feed from my cockpit to the Tas vessel.

I knew from what I had been told by Mitty and Shella that the Tas were quadrupeds, but I didn't see any indication of those appendages in the limited view I had on my screen.

The cilia began to move in a rhythmic pattern and I heard the same mechanical voice speaking to me.

"You are a human?"

"I am."

"You come from a world called Earth?"

"I do."

"Your star has eight primary planets with four rocky worlds orbiting closest to your star. Between the last rocky world and the first of your gas giants there is an asteroid field."

The first statement had been a question. This last was an expression of fact. The question was; How did the Tas know about the makeup of Earth's solar system?

"What you have said is true. May I ask how you knew this when you had never heard of humans?"

The cilia stopped moving. In a few moments they began to undulate again but in a much different pattern.

"This attack was not necessary. You are the lost children of the Ancestors."

Chapter 22: A Dog's Pedigree

"You don't say?" I responded. "Can I assume there is more to this story that you can share?"

"You are unaware of your heritage?" The Tas asked.

"That's an interesting question. If you had asked me yesterday I would have said yes. Given what I've just heard from you; I'm no longer sure. You seemed to recognize my species and you correctly identified my home system. That convinces me you have access to knowledge from a source I don't understand."

"Return to your ship, Admiral Riker. We will no longer attack you. The hive has much to consider before we talk again"

Before I could say more the Taserite closed the channel. I watched as his ship turned around and headed back to his Talon.

In the end, our meeting was less than I had been hoping for but better than I expected. What I hadn't expected was to walk away with yet more questions.

***

I piloted my small shuttle back to the *Gilboa*. I had to admit, I liked seeing her landing bay. A set of undulating landing lights indicated where the Hanger Master wanted me to set the small craft down. As the runners kissed the deck, landing clamps extended out of the floor and locked the shuttle down to the deck firmly. It was a pleasant and reassuring clunk. There had been a time when the ship had seemed very alien to me. Now, it seemed like home.

My wife joined me at the landing bay. To say Lori was pissed with me really doesn't do justice to the word 'pissed'. The only upside to this type of anger was the making up later... My wife was very passionate when it came to 'making up.'

Officially, she was not happy that I had put my life at risk. In reality, she was upset for two reasons. First, I had put my life at risk. Second, and perhaps more importantly, I had done so without talking to her first.

In my defense, I knew I was going. Had I consulted her first, she would be mad that I went and even madder that I had ignored her. Doing it the way I had allowed me to claim the time-honored 'accidently inconsiderate defense.' While this was bad; it was not as bad as blatantly ignoring her concerns.

Fortunately, I was able to extricate myself from a more intense grilling by declaring we needed to have an emergency staff meeting and I wanted her there as the head of medical.

***

"So," I said after I had played the ships automatic data recorder for my senior staff, "we have another series of questions. How did the Tas know about the Sol system? Why did they react to seeing me in the way that they did? And, what is this stuff about 'lost children of the Ancestors'?

The Roharian ambassador walked around the conference table and picked up a bowl of water from the beverage dispenser. The dragons had no use for cups and preferred to drink by lapping water from a deep bowl. As he returned to the table he spoke.

"There is a legend, perhaps more of a myth, among my people. The Ancestors left our region of space after several of their exploration vessels had gone missing. A great darkness was said to have found them. Perhaps humans are the survivors of one such expedition."

Lori leaned forward and spoke.

"I'm not sure I can buy that," she said. "There is a substantial fossil record to support the notion that humanity is from Earth."

Shella looked over at Mitty as if asking for permission to say something. It was the first time in the many months that I had known them that I ever seen any type of deference between the two of them. Mitty nodded.

Shella wrinkled her nose.

"My people have a similar story. The Ancestors were explorers at heart. At various points, their passion for exploration resulted in the loss of some of the explorers. As the story goes once such loss cost the Ancestors their very soul. In the language of the Ancestors, child and soul are synonymous."

We were suddenly getting theological which I wasn't sure was going to be helpful in our current discussion.

"The Ancestor's concept of a soul is fascinating but is it germane?" I asked.

Mitty's wife did that nose-wrinkle thing again.

"You misunderstand me, Admiral. You humans use the phrase 'my family is my heart and soul'. You do not mean to infer your families are your 'actual' heart or your 'actual' soul. You simply are indicating that your family is very precious to you. We believe the same is true about the 'lost children of the Ancestors.'"

I looked over at Lori. Her questions as to the origins of humanity had gone unanswered. I decided to bring that back to the table as it seemed important in putting this question of where humanity came from... and were we, truly, some type of Ancestor offspring?

"Lori's concerns still seem valid. There is strong evidence that Humanity arose from the dust of the Earth. The idea that we were somehow dropped off or stranded on Earth doesn't seem to mesh with the archeological record."

"I might be able to speak to that," Mitty said. "One of the oldest rumors about the Ancestors is that while they came from the core worlds of our galaxy... they did not originate there. It is remotely possible that humanity was the progenitors of the Ancestors rather than the other way around."

***

It took the Taserite Hive three days to deliberate. I was just beginning to think our trip had been a wasted one when my comms officer announced an incoming transmission.

"Open a channel. Audio and video."

A moment later the holographic image of a Taserite appeared about ten feet in front of my command chair. The system was designed to display a life-sized version of the being on the other side.

The creature appeared to be the size and height of a very large dog… say a Saint Bernard or similar large breed. Of course, the Tas looked more like a massive shell-less snail with four very squat legs and a front-facing proboscis capped with the previously mention mouth orifice. They seemed to communicate with each other using rhythmic undulations of the thousands of cilia surrounding that orifice. It also seemed they used their proboscis to manipulate objects much like an elephant uses their trunk.

"Admiral Jeremy Riker," the now familiar mechanical voice said.

"This is Admiral Riker," I responded.

"The hive seeks to speak with the one known as Admiral Jeremy Riker."

"This is he," I answered again. It seemed the Tas had trouble understanding our concept of names. Perhaps they did not use them as such.

"You will forgive me. We struggle with the labels you use for the yet living. Our people lack the full sense of individuality that you do. This has presented us with a difficult and painful choice."

I looked over at my two Ambassadors to see if they could provide any insight. Shelly shook her head. She had become a master of 'human body language.' The Rohar Ambassador just drooled. He caught himself and used a darting tongue to capture the spittle before it hit the deck. It seemed obvious they had nothing to add to the conversation, so I was going to be on my own.

"Please explain this difficult choice you are needing to make," I asked.

"The hive must respond to the Defiler threat and yet we are ill-suited to do so. The lost children of the Ancestors are a far more suitable choice, as the gifts that were placed in our care were left for such as you. We are sending with you a redundant pair. We ask that you do not allow them to become lost children as we grieve their separation from us and yet take comfort in the anticipation of the reuniting. We are a social race. To remove any part is to remove from the whole."

"I think I understand."

"With no disrespect Admiral Jeremy Riker, who is also Admiral Riker... it is unlikely that you do. Nevertheless, the hive appreciates your attempt at understanding. It speaks well of the compassion the Ancestors are known to possess."

"I thank you for sending us these Ambassadors. We were also hoping that you might give us access to a supply of your neutronium missiles. The Defilers seem to have access to a limited amount of Ancestor technology. Our purpose in coming here was to see if we could even the odds a little when we attempt to engage them."

"We will give you unfettered access to all of the gifts that have been left in our care."

I looked up quickly.

"Everybody currently on the bridge. You are to consider the current conversation with the Taserites a class-one secret. Talk to no one about what was said here today under the harshest possible penalties."

As one the bridge crew acknowledged my orders.

"Mitty, you stay. Everybody else clear the bridge."

When they had gone, I turned to face the Archon hologram.

"This may likely be the most important order I ever give you. The fate of the Galactic Order and the fate of my people depend on you keeping it."

"I understand, Admiral. I will seal the previous conversation and the one we are having under an executive lockout. Only you and any you designate will be able to retrieve it."

I nodded and turned back to the Taserite who had been waiting patiently.

"Humanity, and very likely the member worlds of the Galactic Order, would tear themselves apart should such technology come into our hands. Even the knowledge that it could become available... would be devastating. Our societies are not sufficiently advanced to handle the power this technology represents responsibly. It is imperative that you limit our access. The Ancestors trusted you to be guardians. I am asking you to retain that role. Do you understand what I am saying?"

"The hive appreciates and acknowledges your request. That you recognize and accept your own limitations bodes well for your future. We will respect your desire in this matter. Our ambassadors are ready to transport to your ship."

***

It turns out that the Taserite Ambassadors always travel in a pair... and when I say 'always' that's exactly what I mean. The *Gilboa* had received technical specifications for creating living quarters and a mobile environmental unit (MEU) that would allow them to travel throughout the ship.

Their MEU reminded me of those strollers you see in the mall with a set of twins in them. In this case the twins were a pair of two-hundred-pound slugs surrounded by an especially dense transparent shell that enclosed a high-pressure air mix.

That atmosphere contained in both their quarters and the MEU had far more sulfur dioxide than a human could have tolerated even if they could have survived the nearly one hundred bars of pressure. For those that are counting, one hundred bars of pressure is like being a kilometer deep in the ocean. Fine and dandy if you're a sperm whale... a little rough on us homo sapiens.

After the Taserite Ambassadors were onboard and settled in, we received one more transmission from the hive. Our request for advanced missile technology and shielding had been approved. We were to head to a star known as Beta Cancri. It was the home of the Taserite's primary hive. It is there that we were to receive our upgrades.

It is also where we discovered a few unexpected surprises.

Chapter 23: A Bone for the Dog

Beta Cancri was some three-hundred light years from Sol. Fortunately, it was only twenty-three light years from where we had first encountered the Tas. The trip through Skip Space took us a little over a week.

In that time, we learned quite a bit about our newest crew members. As the Taserites did not use names in the same way we did... and because they always traveled together; we took to calling them both Tas... collectively.

The homeworld we were approaching was not the Taserite birth world. That world had been devoured in a supernova many eons ago. What made their new home all the more interesting was that it was in no way suited, environmentally, for the Tas.

The world orbited a relatively young Red Giant that was only about 1.8 billion years old. Beta Cancri was about thirty-four times the size of Earth's Sol but was only 1.7 times the mass. That meant that the nuclear furnace within the star did not burn nearly as hot as Earth's sun.

As a result of the drastically expanded radius but only moderately greater mass, the planets orbiting Beta Cancri did so much closer to the sun's surface. These worlds tended to be exposed to much greater levels of radiation.

The world the Taserite Hive occupied was called Faqqa, which according to Tas meant burst and split world. As we entered orbit, it was immediately clear why the planet had been given that name. The 4,000-kilometer-long Valles Marineris on Mars would be swallowed up many times over in any one of the three major canyons on Faqqa.

The world seemed to be one massive desert... surrounded by more desert... and where there wasn't desert, there was endless expanses of sand. I think you get my point. The atmosphere had been largely eroded by the solar winds. It was about as inhospitable an Earth-sized rocky world could be.

The primary hive occupied a series of impressive pressurized domes that provided protection from the solar radiation as well as a breathable atmosphere... at least according to Taserite standards.

The level of technology required to maintain the domes and protect them from meteorite strikes was well beyond even the level of the Galactic Order. Tas informed us that it was Ancestor technology that kept Taserites safe.

As for why they remained on this God-forsaken world, it was because this was the greatest single concentration of Ancestor artifacts. The Tas were essentially curators and they chose to live near the treasures they protected.

Orbiting the planet were a series of elaborate shipyards and space stations. It was into one of these shipyards that the Tas had us park the *Gilboa*. As big as our ship was, it was dwarfed by the berth we pulled into. I couldn't even imagine the ship that might have filled this bay.

Tas informed us that we would be welcome to debark and enjoy the station. The environmental systems had been designed specifically for the Ancestors... which meant we would be comfortable.

We were informed that the retrofit would take two days and that another week would be required to train the

Gilboa personnel in the operation, repair and upkeep of the new systems.

Unfortunately, it would not be possible to give us the means required to manufacture the neutronium kinetic energy rounds ourselves. We would, however, be supplied with several hundred of the missiles as well as the Higgs field suppression systems required to reduce their mass to a level that could allow them to be easily handled.

Before the Tas could begin the work, the *Gilboa* needed to be evacuated. Installation work would require opening up large parts of the ship to the hard vacuum of space. In addition, per my instructions, there were aspects of the technology used to do the retrofitting that I did not want generally known… even to my own crew.

The J'ni had no problem accepting this order. It was in their nature to defer to the command decisions of others. This was not the case with the human engineers… especially Whiskers.

In the end, I made an appeal to history. In WWII three small countries, Germany, Italy and Japan, took on the rest of the world and almost won. They used technology, developed mostly by the Germans, as a force multiplier.

The Germans were the first to develop long-range missiles. They developed submarines capable of staying submerged for hundreds of miles. They developed a radio navigation system that allowed German night bombers to accurately engage targets without being able to see them. The Germans also developed the most capable jets, night vision systems and numerous other first-of-their-kind weapons systems.

It was only the size and determination of the Allied forces which ultimately outnumbered the Axis forces two to one, that allowed the good guys to have a chance.

Now imagine what would happen if a despot like Hitler were to suddenly have access to technology that wasn't a few years ahead of the rest of the world… but many centuries. Even letting potential despots know that humanity could have access to such technologies would let a genie out of the bottle that would be impossible to put back in.

My friend didn't like it, but he ultimately agreed with the logic.

Lori, Whiskers and I were on the last shuttle to leave the ship. In some ways I felt like a kid going to bed the night before Christmas. I couldn't wait to get up the next morning and see what Santa brought… if Santa was a plethora of two-hundred-pound, poison gas breathing, intelligent slugs.

***

The space station we were dropped off at was… well words could not begin to do it justice.

I've seen more than just about any other human in recorded history. All that said… I was impressed. The technology was so advanced, it almost disappeared. Corridors where lit, with no visible light sources. When we wanted access to a room, a door was there. When we didn't, the door was gone. If I felt cold, the air was suddenly warmer. If I was hungry, there was a food dispenser immediately ahead.

At some point I realized I was tired. A door appeared with a sign above it... Admiral's Suite.

Lori and I spent the next few hours enjoying the sights... without ever leaving the quarters we had been assigned. The suite had six rooms including fully functional kitchen with a replicator the Tas had programmed to duplicate the foods found on the *Gilboa*. The other rooms included an office, a bedroom, a living room, a bathroom bigger than some bedrooms I had slept in... and... a heated swimming pool.

It was obvious that the Ancestors knew how to live! The pool was especially inviting. Lori and I loved to swim but it had been years since we had had the opportunity. Sadly, as we didn't have any swim suits, I expected the pool to go unused. Lori quickly put an end to that thought by shedding her shipsuit and beckoning me to do the same.

Did I mention that my wife had lovely curves in all the right places? I had wanted to explore the rest of the station but there is only so much temptation a man can resist. We frolicked in the water for several hours... and even got some swimming in... amongst other things... did I mention the curves?

After a while we both got hungry... with all the physical activity. Exiting the pool, we spotted folded towels near our folded and cleaned cloths. Thinking that somebody had come in while we were engaged in those things that married couples engage in... Lori turned every shade of red possible. I let her blush for a few minutes before I laughed and told her I had seen a wall panel slide open and service bots come in and do the deed as it were.

She hit me playfully in the shoulder and promised to make me pay for my crimes later... I looked forward to that. They don't call me a dirty old dog for nothing. It had been far too long since we had just enjoyed each other's company and passionate embrace.

Finally, after a few hours' sleep, a nice meal of scrambled eggs and the best synthetic bacon I had ever enjoyed; we decided it was time to meet up with some of the others.

We began to explore the wonders of the rest of the station. Despite the seriousness of our situation, we were having a great time. I hated to admit it, but we needed the down time. I could have hoped that it would last forever. Sadly, that hope faded all too soon.

***

"Will ya look at that," Whiskers said for about the umpteenth time.

The Ancestor station was truly a wonder to behold. My chief engineer had just used a teleportation pad for the first time. It seemed the Ancestors didn't believe in elevators to get from point A to point B. Instead you stepped on a circular oval on the floor.

There were triangular marks on the disks and if you exited the oval over one of these directional arrows you were teleported to another area of the station. The disk you landed on would typically have its own set of directional arrows... including one back to where you came from.

I had made myself dizzy when I discovered you could hop back and forth rapidly on the same set of pads. It seems that human optical nerves (nor my wife for that matter) were not inclined to allow such behaviors without incurring consequences. Translation: I made myself sick and threw up before I realized what had happened. As a side note, the bacon was better the first time through.

Had I not been feeling woozy, I might have been fascinated by how efficiently my vomitus was absorbed by the station's floor.

I was about to suggest Whiskers try the same fast hop trick that I had so much enjoyed when the hall lights turned red and began to thrum. A set of three transportation pads appeared in front of us. Each was circled by undulating red rings. I looked at the others… and stepped onto the nearest pad.

The three of us appeared in what seemed to be a massive control room. A number of MEUs moved about the room. One device moved in our general direction.

"Greetings Admiral Riker. I'm afraid your services will be required a little sooner than anticipated. The Defilers have found us."

***

It seems sometimes you go looking for a fight and other times the fight comes looking for you. This was one of those times.

The Tas had given me a quick, and I do mean quick, overview of the control room and its capabilities. It seemed the Tas were not as well suited to be warriors as they were to be curators.

The automated defense systems could only do so much. Had this invasion happened in a week in either the future or the past, there would have been no issue. A massive cloaking field would have been erected and the wealth of technology on this world and in orbit around it would have gone undetected. Even if the Defilers had attempted to penetrate the cloak, they would have been thwarted by a powerful deflector shield that they would have found impossible to defeat.

That said, the Defilers had arrived at a delicate time when critical components of the *Gilboa's* retrofit were in transit. There was no way to hide the mass of shuttles and supply vessels traveling to and from the planet's surface.

To make matters worse, the Defilers, as we were now calling them, had exited Skip Space where they should not have been able to... half a light minute from Faqqa... impossibly deep within the Beta Cancri gravity well.

For a day that had started off nice enough, it sure had taken a turn for the *not so nice*. While we were still trying to take the measure of the situation, we saw dozens of small attack craft exiting the twenty or so large vessels that just dropped in. This day just kept getting better and better.

Chapter 24: Attack Dog…

"How far can we extend the shields? Can we cover those inbound shuttles?"

"Negative Admiral. They are too spread out," one of the Tas replied. Given the synthetic nature of their voices, it was impossible to tell which one of them was actually speaking. In point of fact, it probably didn't matter. It seemed the Tas, in close proximity to each other, enjoyed a true hive mind… undoubtedly telepathic in nature.

"Can you give me a three-dimensional map of what's going on?" I asked. It was a simple request, but it seemed there were some concepts humans and the Tas were not ever going to be able to communicate to each other. The concept of visualizing something in three-dimensions was one of them.

To their credit, the Tas where very apologetic, but they simply did not understand the nature of the request.

We needed to move on. Time was getting to be critical.

"OK, let's do this. Any ships that are close enough to the shipyard to get under the protection of our shields within the next ten minutes are to proceed. All other craft are to head for the planet's surface, preferably to a surface installation with shielding, but any landing site will do. The key is to get on the ground."

"Orders acknowledged, Admiral," a Tas answered.

"Whiskers, find Colonel Morrison. I need his men in their Mark Ones as soon as possible… preferably yesterday."

"Roger that!"

I looked at Lori.

"See if you can get Mitty and the Ambassadors up here… wherever here is. One of the Tas should be able to help you."

It turned out she didn't need to summon the Archon Hologram. As I turned back around, I about had a heart attack. Mitty had materialized and was floating down to the floor from about six-feet up in the air.

"My pardon, Admiral. The Tas allowed me to transfer my holographic matrix to the station's battle bridge, but unfortunately I had no schematics from which to gage my location."

"No worries my friend. I need you and the *Gilboa's* AI to help me understand the dynamics of what's happening. Work with the Tas to see if you can't get me a three-dimensional display. You may have to simply work with their data feeds and route them through the *Gilboa*."

In less than a minute, Mitty had the display I was looking for. While I had been waiting, I reached out to the Colonel. The Tas had been able to teleport his men's MES and related equipment to the station. They would be suited up and ready to go in fifteen minutes. I told him to make it ten.

I rotated the newly generated holographic display. I could see from the speed of the approaching attack craft that some of the shuttles heading back to the surface where going to be hard-pressed to make a landing in or near the protected zones that had access to Ancestor-grade shields. A few were going to need to make hot landings a good one to two-hundred kilometers away. The fighters were already launching what appeared to be Electro-Magnetic Pulse weapons in a bid to disable some of the shuttles.

It seemed a few of the shuttles, perhaps four, were already compromised. I ordered those ships to bunch up as best they could. I was going to send Mike and his men down to them as fast as I could but there would be a lot of ground to cover if they spread out too far.

"Mitty, do we have anything like point defense weapons we can use to harass those incoming attack craft… give them something to think about besides their prey?"

"Affirmative, Admiral. The station has a comprehensive system for deflecting asteroids."

"Excellent," I said. "It's about time we have some luck. Start giving those attack craft a hard time. Also see if you can target some of those bigger ships with some of those neutronium kinetics energy weapons we have lying about. A good KEW hitting them 'where the sun doesn't shine' should get them rethinking their attack."

I watched as the battle unfolded on two fronts. The asteroid PDS took out about a third of the Defiler's attack ships before they got smart and ducked to the far side of the planet. The bad news was we couldn't hit them anymore. The good news was it gave the pilots of the damaged shuttles a lot more time to get their ships down.

Our neutronium kinetics did a number on the enemy's larger ships. Three of them never saw what hit them. The others jumped into Skip Space before our kinetics got to them. Their ability to enter and exit Skip Space so close to a gravity well was going to be a real headache… but it was a problem for another day.

My suspicion was that the Defilers were after the Ancestor technology that had been destined for the *Gilboa*. The last thing in the world I wanted was for us to hand them yet another advantage. So, I was determined to keep the enemy away from those grounded shuttles that were out in the open.

I discussed options with Mitty and the Tas. After a few minutes I had a plan. Now it was just a matter of seeing if we would have enough time to put it into place.

***

As I said earlier, all but four of the shuttles had made it to the protection of the ground-based shelters. Those four shuttles had taken damage from the Electro-magnetic pulse weapons that the Defilers had fired. The EMPs didn't do serious damage but they did prevent those four shuttles from making it back to the safety of their shielded base.

Sadly, Mitty informed me that these same four shuttles were carrying a handful of the neutronium kinetics and perhaps more importantly, the Higgs field inhibitors needed to use them. These devices effectively allowed mass to be negated. The applications went far beyond advanced kinetics. They could be used to make a small fighter unbelievably maneuverable as well as allowing it to mount massive ablative shields.

At the end of the day… we just didn't want the bad guys to have all the neat toys. They already were playing the game with a seriously impressive and enhanced Skip Drive… I'd be damned if I was going to let them have any more of the good stuff before we had a chance to even the odds.

My biggest worry, at the moment, was those four shuttles out in the middle of nowhere.

It seemed God still had a soft spot in His heart for a sinner like me. I had hoped that the Tas would have some way to teleport my Marines to the surface near those shuttles. I was not disappointed. Each of the shuttles had at least one working teleport pad. That meant Mike's Marines could pop down four at a time – one to each shuttle. They'd, then, have to clear the pad for the next Marine.

It would get the job done but, sadly, it would take time… a full twenty minutes to get an entire company down. That was about ten minutes more that we would need before the Defilers' attack craft rounded the curve of the planet.

We needed some way to buy ourselves some time. The *Gilboa* was still in space dock and wouldn't be leaving anytime soon. The Rohar had very fast, light cruisers that were available to fight but they were vastly outnumbered by the enemy fighters… and vastly out-gunned by the Defiler motherships.

I'd need those ships later. I didn't have a hankering to waste them in a fruitless attempt to take on an adversary they were ill-suited to handle. There had to be another way. I was almost out of ideas… and then I saw Mitty. It's a well-established fact, some of the best ideas come from the strangest of places.

I clicked open my comm-link

"Ambassador Jowls, ready your Roharian Light Cruisers. I have a plan."

* * *

As the Defiler attack fighters rounded the planet and started their dive into Faqqa's atmosphere on a heading that would take them towards the downed transport shuttles... they spotted something that must have given them quite a shock.

The massive *Gilboa* with a light cruiser escort was advancing on the current position of the Defiler motherships. Although the Defiler motherships where outside the range of the neutronium KEWs that the Tas space yard had been firing at them... they were quickly coming in range of the most powerful Galactic Order battleship ever created. One that seemed to be equipped with a number on Ancestor enhancements.

In response, the enemy's motherships engaged their sublight engines and began to run from the approaching *Gilboa* task force.

The Defilers fired round after round of their own KEWs, as well as, plasma beams and antimatter missiles. The *Gilboa* shrugged each of them off. Her shields roiled in an impressive light show but never collapsed. It seemed as if the battleship's defenses were invincible.

The motherships undoubtedly could have entered Skip Space, but it would have meant abandoning their fighters and any potential prizes they may yet wrestle from the Tas.

As expected, the Defiler attack fighters near the planet's surface broke off their planned assault on the downed shuttles and sped off to help in the defense of their motherships.

The entire battle took place over the course of about an hour. The hour was mostly spent chasing one another down. But it was an hour that gave the Marines on the ground a chance to dig in.

As the enemy's fighters arrived in the combat zone they began to engage the Roharian light cruisers. That of course forced the Roharian light cruisers to break their precision formation… and the holographic image of the fake *Gilboa* disappeared. The emitters on the Roharian ships were not powerful enough to maintain the illusion once the formation was broken.

It didn't matter… the ruse had worked. It had bought Mike's Marines the time they needed to get the shuttles and their contents to safety.

The Defiler fleet must have figured they had lost the first round. They backed off and suspended their attack. That said, they did not vacate the system. Translation… we had won round one… but there would be a round two.

***

"How in the hell did they know we were here?" Mike grumbled.

The Colonel was rightfully pissed. It did stretch the bounds of credibility that we would arrive at what had been the heretofore unknown location of the adopted Tas homeworld… at about the same time the enemy… the Defilers… located the Tas.

For the Defilers, this was a motherlode. According to the Tas, there were only a few places in this section of the galaxy that could boast such an abundance of functional, curated, Ancestor technology.

"We need to find out," I agreed. "We also need to figure out what our options are for defending Faqqa. Things would be easier if we had the *Gilboa* in the fight."

"Well, there we have a few options at least," Whiskers said. "The J'ni are crafty little buggers when it comes to moving replacement parts from point A to point B. They've put together a system with the Tas to teleport the pieces we need for the *Gilboa's* upgrades directly up to the station. It will take a week or more just to get the various retrofit components together. It's a lot slower than using the transport shuttles… but it will get the job done."

"We have one more priority," I said. "I'm tired of not knowing who we are fighting. Come hell or high water… I want to capture one of those smaller Defiler attack ships and have a heart-to-heart conversation with its crew."

I didn't know it at the time, but I was to learn… the hard way… that sometimes knowledge is its own worst enemy.

Chapter 25: Presents for the Dog

Three days later the Defilers were still hanging out in the Beta Cancri system. They had slowly drifted to a position some 6AU out from Faqqa. The retrofit on the *Gilboa* was proceeding... not fast... but it was proceeding.

Mike, Whiskers and a handful of J'ni that were not engaged in the work on the *Gilboa* were doing their own retrofits on the combat fighters that had been in the *Gilboa's* fighter bay. With the permission of the Tas, they had fitted about half of the little ships with the Higgs Field inhibitors.

The Higgs boson generates the field which gives objects their mass. In theory, completely nullifying a Higgs field would allow a ship to achieve velocities approaching the speed of light. Our devices were not capable of that, but they could reduce the effective mass of our ships by over ninety percent. That translated into more shields, more weapons and more speed. This was definitely a case where more was better.

Our worries about protecting the planet from an expected Defiler attack turned out to be less critical. The Tas presented me with two surprises while we metaphorically waited for the other Defiler shoe to drop.

The Archon Ambassador, Shella, Mitty, Lori and I were 'summoned' by the Tas. I was on the *Gilboa's* bridge reviewing the integration of new systems as the aforementioned systems were being brought online. We still had quite a bit of work to be done but at least we had functional shields, limited sublight propulsion and a handful of enhanced weapon systems available. It would be another day until we had our planned KEW upgrades and two before we had our new Skip Drive operational. The one plus side to the way we were doing the upgrades now... was that my crew was an active part of the work and thus were learning on the job how to service and maintain the new systems. The Tas had even given us a new library of service routines for our Da'Tellen teaching devices.

At any rate, the four of us received the summons via a holographic messenger that suddenly appeared before each of us. If you've never had a pony-sized giant slug appear three feet in front of you... let me just say... it can get your heart racing. Each received the exact same cryptic message... 'Come Now.'

As the *Gilboa* was now fitted with a very large teleport pad that was used to move cargo to and from the *Gilboa* and the space dock, we attempted to use it to pop over to the station. I say attempted, because while we did teleport... it just wasn't to the space station.

To say the room, we arrived in, was massive or even cavernous was to do an injustice to the terms 'massive' and 'cavernous.' You could fit an entire city into the space... and here's the thing. I was to learn that if we had arrived three days before... there would have been a Taserite city here.

Now, it was completely and absolutely empty. I suspected you wouldn't even be able to hear an echo. The walls, such as they were... were simply too far apart.

The atmosphere had been replaced with something that we could breathe and at a pressure we could tolerate. That, in itself, was an engineering marvel.

"OK, that's not what I was expecting," I said to the group.

"Where are we?" Lori asked.

I had a suspicion but before I could say anything, Mitty who was transmitting his holographic image from a mobile emitter connected to a belt his wife was wearing, spoke up.

"I believe we are in a Taserite dome city on the planet's surface. I find it intriguing that the city itself is no longer here."

"Intriguing... yes, that's exactly the word that came to my mind," I said with just a touch of friendly sarcasm.

The teleport pad vibrated the tiniest bit. We had learned that this was its polite way of asking people to vacate the pad, so a subsequent teleportation could occur. As we stepped off the pad, it shimmered, and a large number of objects appeared. One of the items looked suspiciously like a status pod. It was much smaller than the ones we had on the *Gilboa* and seemed to have a lot more flashy-light-things on it.

At the same time a second hologram materialized. I knew it was a hologram because, just like on the *Gilboa*, it was a Tas... minus the environmental support units required to support it in a human-friendly environment.

"Greeting Admiral Riker. As you can see, our diaspora is complete. The hive that made this world home is now many parsecs away and is safe."

"That's great," I said.

If I had had any doubts about the level of technological superiority that the Ancestors represented... they were squashed. There was no way humanity could handle power of this magnitude at our current level of cultural advancement. The old adage about absolute power corrupting absolutely kept running through my mind.

"What about your people still on the station?" Lori and Shella asked in unison... which, if I'm honest – I have to admit, was pretty freaky given that the two of them were not even of the same species... just say'n.

"They will join us when their task is done."

The holographic Tas paused before continuing. There was almost a tinge of remorse in its synthetic voice.

"Admiral, we believe you represent the best hope for the future of this region of space. That said, we cannot allow you to know our current location. Although we do not hold you personally responsible... we believe your ship was culpable of sharing our location with the Defilers.

"The devices on the transport platform will allow you to contact us. Use them sparingly as their energy stores are not inexhaustible. In addition, we have provided several items that will aid you in your quest to end the reign of the Defilers within the Galactic Order."

The holographic Tas shifted to the side, as only a two-hundred-pound slug can, to stand in front of the two Archons.

"We bring you a gift as well. Although we cannot and will not force you to accept the gift, we believe it is essential to the ultimate success of your mission. It also represents a new future for your people."

"Gift?" Shella asked.

"In the germination pod you will find a male husk of your species. It was adapted from your genetic material. The husk has been fashioned to resemble your biological mate. Its genome has been enhanced to remove any aberrant code sequences. The germination pod, if used during gestation, will provide for sufficient genetic diversity to safely reestablish your species."

I stepped forward. The Tas had said something the concerned me greatly.

"When you say 'husk', just what exactly to you mean?"

"The husk was fabricated without a cerebral cortex. It is capable of normal autonomic activities, but it is not self-aware. Imbedded within its chest cavity is a cybernetic brain that is capable of accepting the engrams stored on your vessel from her husband."

"You intend to bring me back from the dead," Mitty said in something between wonder and horror.

"It might be better to think of our gift as a biological avatar. Although it will look like your progenitor, you will remain your own entity. You will remain connected with the *Gilboa's* AI should you chose to be. In addition, your avatar will be functional in those areas required for procreation."

Mitty looked at Shella. He had holographic tears in his eyes.

"We can't do it. As much as I want to be alive and to hold you in my arms… it won't be me... It won't… be… me," Mitty said sadly.

"Shut up you fool," Shella said fiercely. "Will it be the husband I buried? Certainly not, but it will most certainly be you... an entity I have grown to love over these many months. You will accept this gift and that is the end of it."

With that business out of the way, the Tas once again faced me.

"The hive has one final request of you Admiral Riker. We would ask that you destroy this planet."

***

An hour later I was briefing my command staff on my final meeting with the Tas. I had to admit, as meetings go... this last one with the Tas had been amongst the strangest... especially the last request.

Lori had been given a full set of specs on the germination pod... this was curtsey of another Da'Tellen brain download. She assured me that she could build one of the things by the time the memory dump was complete. That was good because we only had one Archon husk to work with and it didn't look like we would be getting any more in the near future. I wasn't sure how Shella would react should the transfer fail and the husk be damaged.

The work on the *Gilboa* would be sufficiently complete that we could leave the space dock in about a day. At that time, I was to issue a command that would cause devices planted deep within the planet's mantle to begin a countdown to detonation. These devices were sizable containers of antimatter. The resulting explosion would rival a nova and destroy everything within several AU of the planet. The blast would be so strong, there was a 16% chance it would destabilize Beta Cancri for a number of years.

Our new Skip Drive was going to be able to jump near gravity wells in a manner very similar to our Defiler friends. This was fortunate since I had no particular desire to be engulfed in the big bang we were going to set off on our way out of dodge.

I still had the goal of capturing one of the enemy. Fortunately for us, the enemy was more than happy to accommodate us.

My buddy Colonel Mike Morrison had been working on a plan to accomplish this goal. All we needed was for our friends to come-a-courting again. Soon enough the red-alert klaxon sounded.

I raced for the bridge along with the rest of the command staff. Mitty met us on the turbo-lift.

"Admiral, we have detected eighty-four jump points forming. It would appear that the enemy is massing for an attack."

"Are they as close as before?" I asked.

"Negative, Admiral. They are entering the system considerably further out. It's possible these ships are not equipped to jump deeply into a gravity well."

I nodded in relief. Our plans were predicated on having a day to get the ship put back together. Capturing one or more of the Defilers would be pointless if we ended up being nothing more than so much dust floating around in space. I knew in my heart, that at the end of the day... I would detonate the planet, whether we were still in orbit or not, to keep the Defilers from gaining access to any more

Ancestor tech... and that included the space dock and station in orbit around Faqqa.

***

"Decoupling locking clamps," Commander Shelby reported. "Station keeping thrusters have us stabilized. Secondary shields are online. Beginning to back out of space dock. Positioning thrusters at ten percent. Higgs field dampeners operating within expected range."

"Very good, Number One. Mike, as soon as we clear the bay, bring our primary shields online."

"Aye, aye, Admiral," Mike said with a casual salute for emphasis.

I didn't like people saluting me... especially while on the bridge. The Marine Commander knew this and so he offered the salute as a whimsical way of teasing a friend. I was tempted to return his salute, using a single finger, but I decided it would be unbecoming the Galactic Order's only active-duty Fleet Admiral.

"Sensors, what's the status of our friends out there?" I said instead.

"All one-hundred and two enemy ships are advancing on our position at zero-point-one percent light-speed. They should be within weapons range in just under eighteen minutes, Sir."

"Very good. Keep me updated in case the situation changes."

I turned towards the Engineering station and Whiskers. I could tell from his broad grin that our little surprise was ready.

Chapter 26: Dog Catcher

When the *Gilboa* was several hundred kilometers away from the space dock, I put the first part of our plan into motion. Carefully placed charges on the exterior hull of the station exploded in a very specific sequence. A number of the charges that had been placed appeared to have failed or only partially detonated. These too were part of the master plan. I was going to miss that pool and the good times Lori and I had had in it. Such be the fortunes of both love and war.

The space dock slowly deorbited and crashed into the planet's surface. Given the nature and durability of the Ancestor technology, it was highly likely that much of the advanced tech survived the descent and subsequent impact... which was just the way we wanted it.

Imagine tossing a steak on the ground to catch the attention of a guard dog... same principle.

To cement the trap, I had Mike launch a flight of our enhanced fighters with orders to strafe the wreckage on the ground. Of course, our guys were using old-fashioned chemical munitions. They would kick up a lot of dust and dirt, but not much else. Our steak would remain good and juicy.

As predicted, the Defilers launched their own fighters. I love it when a plan comes together. Our guys... the ones that had been engaged in the strafing runs... quickly climbed back into orbit to engage the enemy.

Our new birds were considerably more agile than the enemy's ships. In addition, they could take a pretty serious punch and not be down and out. In fact, we only had two casualties, and neither one of them was fatal. The same could not be said about the Defiler's fighters.

Our new fighter KEWs were based on the same Higgs Field technology as the neutronium weapons. In this case however, they enhanced the effective mass of a steel-tipped KEW just prior to impact.

We took out forty of their fighters in short order. It sounds impressive but keep in mind, the bad guys had over a hundred mother ships of varying sizes. Between them, they had over three hundred of their fighters in the air… with more launching every minute.

It was time to put the final piece of our plan into motion. I toggled the ship-to-ship comms.

"Gentlemen, put operation 'Dog Catcher' into motion."

"Roger that, Admiral."

The speaker was none other than one of our ace pilots, a rogue by the name of JM Robison, a.k.a 'the Jam man'.

"We have our net out and waiting for a little doggie to stop by."

The net in this case was a set of cloaked microsatellites that each contained two components: a radio and a powerful Higgs Field generator. Rather than inhibit a Higgs Field, they operated like our smaller enhanced KEWs and increased the effective mass of anything that came within their effective field of operation. To make things more exciting for any little doggies that fell into our trap… the field generators were set to toggle on and off at the rate of about ten times a second.

Imagine sitting in a metal wheelbarrow being pushed down a rough gravel road while having a couple hundred pounds of cinderblocks resting on your chest. Think… uncomfortable. Our goal was to incapacitate whoever or whatever was piloting any Defiler craft we were fortunate enough to catch.

My biggest worry was that we were constrained by the clock. I had given the planetary destruct order once the *Gilboa* cleared the space dock. That gave us a hard deadline to vacate the system in thirty minutes. We had already burned through twenty of those. In forty minutes, the Beta Cancri system was not going to be a place you wanted to be.

I told Mike to get his Marines back on the boat or they were going to be left behind. Five minutes from our deadline everybody was back on board except for the Jam Man. It seemed at the last minute he had a stray wander into his trap. What the Higgs Field Inhibitor taketh away… the Higgs Field Enhancers giveth back.

Eight minutes later a very concerned Admiral was pleased to hear that both dog catcher and little doggie were safely onboard. I issued the final order I ever would in this particular star system.

"Punch it Chewie."

We entered Skip Space shortly before the biggest explosion to ever occur in this region of space consumed an entire world and slightly over one-hundred ships belonging to an enemy we had never met face to face. But, that at least, was about to change.

***

"Crack 'er open," Colonel Morrison ordered. I was watching the grand unveiling from behind a class three force screen. Mike had flat out refused to let me get any closer. Mike and his team were geared up in Combat MEUs.

Mitty, being a hologram... at least for the moment, was safe to watch from a position right next to the Marines. Through the magic of technology, that I wouldn't even have been able to dream of when I graduated from the Space Academy, a group of us beyond the force-field watched the events unfold through Mitty's holographic eyes. This group included Lori, Whiskers, Shella, Shelby and myself.

The Defiler craft had been secured. A second, far more powerful forcefield, isolated the alien fighter from the rest of the ship... on the off chance it blew up.

Every effort to communicate with the occupants of the ship was met with silence. With no other choice, the decision was made to force an entry into the ship.

Mike's team had been trained in this type of operation. Two of his bigger guys brought out what was affectionately called the can-opener. Think of it as a 'jaws of life' on steroids. They made short order of the singular man-sized hatch that we had found in the ship.

With a clang that could be heard throughout the hanger, the hatch fell away. Mike quickly entered the craft with his weapon drawn.

The longest two minutes of my life later the Marine exited the craft and walked over to my position.

"They're all dead," he said dryly. "And Admiral, *they're human.*"

Epilog

Three weeks later, the *Gilboa* was finally completely operational. Mitty had a new organic body and we had solved one great mystery only to have discovered a bigger one.

Where had the Defilers come from? While it was true that they were originally of human stock, analysis of their genome showed a thirty percent hybridization with Neanderthal DNA.

Somehow, in Earth's distant past, aliens had visited our planet and made off with some of her inhabitants. The whys and hows remained a mystery. From our perspective, uncovering our enemy and discovering we were distant cousins was sobering.

In some ways the news was good. I had every expectation that we would have a much better idea of how our adversaries thought… knowing they probably thought and reacted like us. On the other hand, it was disconcerting to learn the depths of depravity to which our kind could stoop.

Of course, the final question… the one that would take me the better part of a year to even ask was… Who was pulling the strings behind the scene? I wouldn't like the answer.

*** This ends War Dog ***

Dog's Adventures will continue in book number 2, "Mad Dog"

Check out my other SCIFI series:
The Catherine Kimbridge Chronicles (9 books)
The Infinity Brigade (3 books)

Made in the USA
San Bernardino, CA
16 February 2019